THE HIGHWAY

BY
LELDE KOVALOVA

First published in Latvia in 2021 by "Latvijas Mediji"
Translator: Elyatha Eli
Cover design: Natalie Kugajevska, Lelde Kovalova

i

To Daniel,

When you were five years old,
the world fought a dangerous virus,
and you and I were isolated.
It was in the distant 2020s.
Back then, I wrote this novel,
but you were preoccupied with puzzles.

With love,
Mom

CHAPTER ONE

It is said that women—like cats—have a premonition of danger. Cats have paranormal capabilities to sense fire and even natural disaster—an earthquake or the eruption of a volcano. Women can also be aware of accidents long before the threat becomes real.

That night, I was tormented by the worst dream I had ever had Only at dawn, I could set it aside in the corner of my consciousness. When I woke up, I felt a drop of blood trickling from my nose. The realization that the experience was just a terrible dream allowed me to calm down. The nightmare seemed genuinely terrifying . . . It felt as if my mind had flown away and left the body as an empty shell.

As I glanced outside the second-floor bedroom window, I saw thick swatches of mist sliding across the fields, ambushing the dry ash trees in the courtyard and the twin rows of houses in the distance.

We live near the highway but in almost complete isolation from the outside world. Opposite to us, there is another private house that has been vacant for many years. A rural road two kilometers long leads to the highway, and the row of tasteless twin houses linger at its end. Almost nobody lives in them. My husband thinks it is insane to buy real estate built near highways. Besides, those hideous boxes cost astronomically.

I climbed out of bed and went to the bathroom. As I glanced in the mirror, a pale face looked back at me—glossy from the mixture of my night cream and sweat. My eyes were dull, but the strands of dark hair were damp on my forehead, tousled to all sides. I washed my face with cold water and scrubbed the dried blood from my upper lip. It made me feel a little better, enough to get dressed and head downstairs.

The house was incredibly silent, and the only sound was the ticking clock on the wall. As usual, my husband's desk was drowned under piles of document folders. There was no sign of Agris. Perhaps he left to work earlier than usual this morning? I overslept—maybe that's why I hadn't met him.

Dodger dashed into the living room. He is our dog and a beloved member of our family. He is a sand-colored Labrador retriever with an incredible intellect and good-natured temperament.

We took him from the animal shelter because his previous owner had moved abroad, and there hadn't been a plane ticket to the new home for the man's "best friend."

"Dodger, where's Agris?" I ruffled the Labrador's ears, and the dog whined in satisfaction. As he wriggled his tail, Dodger led me into the kitchen. After filling his food bowl, I remained by the window. A view to the outdoor terrace unfolded before me, and Agris was already sitting there by the table, sipping his morning coffee and studying messages that kept scrolling on the screen.

Agris is a successful man. My husband is a director of a logistics company dealing with cargo transportation in Europe and the former Republics of the Soviet Union. It is a stressful job because freights worth thousands of euros often get stuck on the borders for several days. Agris successfully leads the company's logistical specialists, preventing both staff fraud and reduction in the company's turnover in all circumstances, even the most difficult ones.

From the terrace, you could see the large courtyard and the path to the forest behind it. The house and fifty hectares of the land belonged to my father until my parents announced they would live in an apartment in Riga and offered us this property as a wedding gift.

Father now enjoys the peaceful life of his retirement, but from time to time, he invests sometime in the real estate market, buying and selling apartments to ordinary citizens. Mother spends her days polishing windows and baking cakes on weekends because she worked as a confectioner all her life, and she was unable to give up her favourite hobby even after retirement.

I grew up here. I know every stomp in the meadow behind the yard up to the forest. I remember every scratch in the plaster outdoors, scraped in the walls during my childhood. I love this clay-yellow brick house with the dark brown ranilla roofing, the wide windowsills and the old wood vines on the fence.

In the early eighties, the municipality allocated one of the three flats in this house to my father as he was the new land reclamation specialist. In 1994, when the home was returned to its owners, and it was no longer advantageous for the other two families to live here, my father brought this house and called it the Woodwalks. It became our family's nest for many years. We didn't really live in the apartment in Riga—it was only there to work, study or stay overnight after a theatre show or after visiting our friends.

Father gave me the Woodwalks shortly before my wedding. Agris acknowledged my parents' wedding gift as royal and took time to enrich it. He was passionate about building the terrace, mowing the lawn, and frequent jogging in the nearby forest. Agris grew up in an orphanage because his parents lost their custody rights. My husband fell in love with this house as his own. However, he didn't want to accept the house as a gift, and my mother recently blabbed that he had transferred my father an impressive amount of money— equal to the prices in the real estate market—not long after our wedding.

"Morning, sleepy!" Agris turned his head in my direction and called me to sit down. I noticed that my man's face looked tired too. He had been working a lot lately, and dark circles formed under his eyes, making him appear exhausted.

"I had a terrible sleep and disgusting nightmares," I said, kissing my husband's forehead.

Dodger cocked his head and looked at us with valiant eyes, glancing at my husband, then me and wiggling his tail in satisfaction.

The tall ash tree trio on the side of the yard looked

sorrowful. It had developed a parasitic disease that had destroyed plenty of Latvian trees in recent years. The large coarse branches reached for the sky, leaving detached flakes of bark detached from the branches.

I turned my gaze sideways to the meadows behind the yard, where the pathway trickled towards the forest. It kept fading in the distance—at first, seeming thin and almost sweet, but the edge of the forest hid thick and mighty fir trees and pine trees. I hadn't visited that forest since I was seven. Childhood memories of the unforgettable event still haunted me.

"Do you have time to have breakfast with me?" I asked my husband.

"Yes, of course. I have to leave in an hour."

"I'll prepare some breakfast," I smiled.

"Thank you." Agris stroke my back gently, leaving his hand on my waist for a moment longer. His gaze returned to the computer screen.

The Labrador chose to come with me because between Agris and I—he always chose food and warmth.

For breakfast, I prepared eggs and bacon, sliced avocados. It was my husband's favourite meal, and he liked routine. Agris used to say that the key to success was based on daily habits, persistence and discipline. He enjoyed reading self-help books written by Napoleon Hill, Robin Sharma and similar prophets. Agris worked out every morning, although he enjoyed his evening jogging with Dodger more.

My husband and I don't have much in common. I enjoy adventures, but the routine makes me bored. Instead of yoga and jogging, I would rather choose to read novels about Latvians—the eternal sufferer. I should probably start exercising, although I had successfully avoided physical activities for thirty years. Instead of having long walks in the evenings, I usually choose a glass of white wine and a movie on Netflix.

We have been happily married for six months, and I feel lucky. Agris isn't the type of a man found in sentimental novels. Like any of us, he has his own weaknesses—but he works hard for the family, hardly consumed any alcohol, and we rarely argue. We have known each other for almost two years, and we live in harmony and happiness.

During our breakfast, we enjoyed the advantages of having a private house and an outdoor terrace.

"What are your plans for today?" Agris asked, turning to me.

"I'll try to do something useful," I replied, making it clear that I didn't want to talk about what was planned yet. I didn't enjoy the idea that I had no 'to-do' list in the early morning.

"Do you still remember about the evening?" I mentioned, suddenly worried that my husband would have forgotten about the upcoming guests.

"I know, I know. Paula and her new guy." Agris put a slice of avocado in his mouth and smiled. Is he really going to be *the one and only* for her?"

"Maybe." I smiled, remembering who many *the one and only's* I had seen. "Be merciful towards him. By the way, he is a demanded fitness trainer!"

"What do you think—will he eat meat?" Agris asked in

all his seriousness. "I was unsure how to react when Paula introduced us to her previous boyfriend, who began exclaiming how much suffering the turkey had to go through before it got delivered to our table."

"Agri!" I chuckled, remembering the precious cupid. That love story dissolved from my sister's life as quickly as any other of her boyfriends. A new crush has appeared in her life, and she wants us to meet him in the evening.

The upcoming dinner made me anxious. Sister had a successful career. Maybe that's why she was never worried about her *the one and only's* occupations. Paula was the head of the airline's security department, and her income was well above the average salary in Latvia. Unlike Paula, I was unemployed, and it sometimes drove me to despair. There were other reasons why I didn't want the upcoming dinner, but I feared to even think about them. I was afraid to become even more depressed.

Agris earned money and paid our bills. A month before our wedding, I found out that the printing house where I worked would close and dismiss their staff. It shattered me because I loved my job. On a daily basis, I was responsible for cooperation with book publishers, and my projects were mainly related to fiction publishing. I indulged in every novel, the path of publishing every bit of poetry, felt excited about the book covers, layouts and typographical errors. Beautiful books made me feel delighted each time I stroked their covers. After losing my job, I was going to apply for vacancies in other publishing houses, but the worries of wedding preparations took all my time, so I missed out on the job seeking.

After that, I officially became unemployed, and I agreed with Agris' suggestion no to return to work because we were planning to have a baby.

"See you in the evening, darling," Agris finished his breakfast, quickly grabbed the computer from the desk and kissed my forehead before leaving.

"Have a good day!" I smiled and escorted him to the hallway, where he kissed me once more after getting dressed—this time on my lips.

When we went outside on the porch, warm spring rays of light caressed us, shining brightly with the first beams of October. The mist seemed scattered. A few fluffy clouds painted the light blue sky.

Agris got into the car, waved at me, started the engine and drove to the road. The car picked up the speed and quickly disappeared towards the highway.

I was left alone again.

And just as usual, it scared me a little.

CHAPTER TWO

In the afternoon, the weather changed rapidly. The clouds behind the window became gloomy and fiercely tried to lie down on the dry grass. The area seemed wrapped in some cotton wool. The sunny day turned into cold fog. The grey sky, our yellowish house with the brown roof and the view of the ash trees—those were turning into my daily routine twenty-four hours a day, seven days a week. I rarely went out. I simply had no errands to run since I was unemployed.

Agris had probably already solved the logistics issues, but I only sipped my second cup of coffee and looked outside the living room window towards the only nearby building in the area where a new neighbour had recently moved in. The house used to be vacant for years, but a few months ago, a forty-year-old woman bought the house. I had noticed that every morning, she would go somewhere in her Passat, but the car would be back at her place in the afternoons.

Not long ago, enjoying the taste of the late raspberries, I came to a conclusion—every time I went outside to the garden, the neighbor would also appear in her backyard.

Every time I stayed in the kitchen or the living room for a while longer, the woman would glance outside her window. As if accidentally looking towards the road, she would peek in the direction of my house. Whenever I would go out, she did the same at the very exact moment. Ironically, she seemed to have her afternoon coffee on her terrace at the same time as I had mine.

"There must be a logical explanation," Agris laughed as I shared the strange observations. "She definitely wants to meet you! Both of you stay in this lonely neighborhood day-to-day. You know, I think you should go and make friends with that lady."

"I'm surprised it didn't occur to me earlier," I admitted to my husband. "I've also noticed that she rarely goes outside her house. Tomorrow, I'll go and introduce myself to the mysterious neighbor."

Suddenly, I felt overwhelmed with the idea.

"Just don't get too excited about the ladies' nights out," Agris chuckled and reached out his hands towards me. "In the evenings, you belong to me only. Do we have a deal?"

"I promise," I replied and smiled in return.

Meeting my neighbor happened recently, and it didn't turn out quite as I had planned.

After opening the door to answer my determined attempts to ring the doorbell, she seemed so surprised that she had lost her ability to speak for a moment. The woman frowned at me, spared me an unsatisfied glance and crossed her arms over her chest as if to protect herself with an embrace.

"How can I help you?" she asked as I stood on her porch with a homemade pie in my hands. Suddenly, I felt like a complete idiot.

"I just wanted to meet you," I gathered my courage to blab the words. Only afterwards, I realized how foolishly I had acted, disturbing a stranger with my presence. There were many introverts in the world who disliked unexpected company, and I was ignorant enough not to consider it before surprising my neighbor with my sudden arrival. Perhaps she was one of them, enjoying her quiet and peaceful life in the cave called 'home'.

"This is for you," I said, handing her the pie awkwardly. I wished I could leave as soon as possible.

"Thank you. It's very nice of you," she replied coldly, grasping the ornate melchior tray with the pie on it. There was no slightest hint that I would be welcomed to enter her house, not even for a moment. I was hoping to get my tray back after the neighbor would invite me for a cup of tea, but I realized that it didn't seem to cross her mind at all. The woman's voice was tense, but her green eyes were the darkest shade of moss, and her skin was flawlessly smooth. Maybe she was under forty years old, aster all? It was impossible to tell, considering how many women drunk collagen pills and had their fillers done nowadays?

"If we can ever help you somehow, please feel free to visit us," I added politely and was about to leave.

I walked away, putting my feet in the previously made markings of my steps that were still visible on the lawn. It seemed as if the sun radiated unusual light, illuminating the tree branches too sharply and making the pathways on the yard appear narrower than they truly were.

"Thank you, Laura," the woman followed me quickly when I had gone a few steps further away from her.

I turned around sharply. I stopped and froze.

"Excuse me, what did you say?" I asked disbelievingly.

The woman frowned again as if trying to understand what I wanted from her.

"How did you know my name?" I was pretty sure we had never introduced ourselves to each other before.

"I've probably heard your name while tending the garden," the woman quickly noted. "My name is Aya," she added.

Was it only my imagination, or did her face really pale? Although, why would it? Her answer was reasonable—our houses were relatively close, and she could've easily heard the disputes between Agris and me through her window.

"I'm pleased to meet you, Aya!" I said and walked away as quickly as I could.

"Thanks for the pie! It looks lovely!" The neighbor's voice came from behind me, but I no longer dared to look back.

CHAPTER THREE

After drinking another cup of coffee, I relaxed in the comfortable armchair in the living room, wondering how to fill my day. I wanted to avoid having another meaningless twenty-four hours. A book from my father's library sat in my hands, but during the first page, my gaze involuntarily slid towards the neighbour's house, which seemingly sparkled through my living room window.

I was unsure what exactly I tried to see there because the woman was usually away during this time of day. I had no clue where she worked, what she did at all, but there were numerous strange things about my neighbour:

She lived alone and was shut in her own bubble.

Sometimes, she behaved oddly.

I used to wonder—why was I so interested in my neighbour? Was it because my life was so quiet and predictable? It was so happy that I felt bored at times.

Almost six months have passed since my wedding. Agris and I live in the seventh heaven of our first year of marriage, and we wish to have a baby. I'm thirty-two, and Agris will turn thirty-five in spring—both of us are enjoying our best years. We own a house in the countryside, and my husband has a stable income.

Why do I feel so bothered? I'm not sure what worries me more—the fact that I'm still unemployed or that I haven't conceived a baby. Agris insisted that I don't look for a job. New work would come with new responsibilities and stress, and his income was enough to let me remain a housewife. If I got pregnant, I'd have to leave the job at some point, anyway. Everything indicated that it was best for me to wait for the pregnancy test to bless my husband and me with two stripes.

Sometimes, I feel like no one needs me. Agris' phone rings even when he's at home, and he would answer his e-mails on weekends and holidays during the mornings. My husband claims to hate it as much as I do. He says he would rather spend his time off with no signal or an internet connection, but that is impossible.

I, on the other hand, rarely have any calls. Agris calms me by saying that, nowadays, everyone is too busy with their social media and various apps—and even then, they rarely leave any messages. Perhaps he is right. I don't talk to my friends too often either. Our conversations are more like formal phrases for the sake of politeness rather than proper communication. Usually, we speak only to catch up with the events missed during a year of not meeting up for a cup of tea.

Mother calls me once a week. When I worked in typography, I would come up with multiple excuses not to talk to her—I never had any time. It was true, though.

I lack any ideas to offer to Agris when he comes home after work and asks me about my evening plans. I spend my days watching TV series, tidying the house and stalking our neighbour. No, I'm not ungrateful nor unhappy! Not at all! After all, I have an attractive husband, financial stability, a friendly dog, a private house and... I have quite an attractive face.

I have it all on the days when I don't see any nightmares due to the stress about being unemployed and seeing negative pregnancy tests.

My life is simple. I have no unplanned events—good nor bad. Neither small nor big.

"Perhaps you should return to work?" Mother recently mentioned on a phone call. "You used to love it so much. I'm sure the managers of other printing houses would be pleased to have you as an employee, considering your experience."

"Mom, I know!" I replied. "But Agris wants a baby, and so do I! We feel ready for it. I'm afraid that the stress at work would sabotage our plans."

"Nonsense!" Mother exclaimed. "Children come when they come. Your generation wants to receive everything on some ridiculous deadlines."

We hadn't received the two stripes on the pregnancy tests as expected during the half a year of our marriage, so we went through various examinations. They confirmed that we were healthy and my eggs were ready for a battle. I promised myself not to obsess over the delays in pregnancy. Instead, I tried to relax and let the baby arrive on its own terms. However, the awareness that for a woman in the best years of my life—in my thirties—I was useless not only in my career but also in my family life. It depressed me, planting awful thoughts in my mind.

I tried focusing on the book to eliminate the upsetting thoughts and turn my attention to other people's problems. And again—without realising it—I looked up towards the window. It almost made me jump in fright. Through the thin curtain web, I saw my neighbour watching me. One of the second-floor windows of the opposite house was open, and the woman stood there—tall like a candlestick, motionless like a statue. I felt a sudden tingling sensation in my fingertips, and it seemed as if the same wave of electric current passed throughout both of us. Nothing like it had ever happened to me. The neighbour was acting odd, and it started seriously bugging me.

I got up and went closer to the window to draw the clay-white curtain open. It gave me a clearer picture of her. For a while, the neighbour continued eyeing me as if I were a ghost. However, she turned away and disappeared from the view a moment later. Why would she do that?

She would always study me—what was she trying to find? I suspected that she was lonely and suffered from depression. Once, I had read that continuous solitude could not only make people feel ill but even turn a person into a murderer. Long ago, scientists had already admitted that loneliness was a disease, not a choice—that humanity was under a threat of epidemic loneliness. They believed it would cause severe health crisis and become the reason for many deaths.

I felt sorry for the woman. She lived utterly alone—perhaps her husband was dead, or she couldn't have any children. On the other hand, all of it was just my imagination. I took a step away from the window and promised myself that I wouldn't follow my neighbour's business for the rest of the day.

At that moment, it didn't even cross my mind that her plan could be similar.

CHAPTER FOUR

Agris' car showed up by our house before eight o'clock. It was earlier than usual. Sometimes he would arrive home only after ten o'clock when I was ready to go to bed.

I felt already exhausted although the guests hadn't arrived yet. Paula called half an hour ago to announce that they will come after eight.

I had cooked a marinated chicken with vegetables and my husband's favourite Teriyaki sauce. It was one thing I could prepare flawlessly. For the dessert, we had Beze cookies and chocolate fondue. The house was spotless as I had scrubbed every corner half of the day. I was incredibly excited about the guests that would dismiss the loneliness of the evening.

Later, I had a shower, and I got dressed in a lovely dress, braided my hair like a young girl—it made me look innocent and cute.

As soon as Agris noticed me, he shook his head, grinned and pulled me closer to him.

"You look fantastic!" He kissed me on my lips.

Dodger wriggled his tail next to us, and Agris ruffled the dog's ears as he always would as soon as he came home. I loved viewing this scenery. Sometimes, I imagined how I would meet my husband with the baby, and a little while later, our child would run towards his dad as soon as the lights of Agris' car appeared by the roadway.

Paula and her new boyfriend—George—arrived a moment after Agris, and both dashed into the house playfully. As soon as George removed his jacket and remained in the tight t-shirt, his occupation was clear as daylight. The sturdy torso was wrapped in great muscles, making the man look like a fictional character from the cartoons with superheroes. His brawny arms were especially worthy of the attention as he held an adorably tiny bouquet of roses before the superman handed it to me gallantly. George looked unnecessarily worried and overly masculine, but he looked like a matching pair to my persuasive sister. Paula's dark hair messily curled to all sides, but I also knew that it had to be the latest fashion trend. My sister was dressed comfortably—she wore a cotton blouse, skinny jeans and classic black shoes. I noticed that George kept smiling at her—it had to be the cause for Paula's melting heart. At some point, the fitness charmer secretly slid his hand down Paula's back, resting it on her softest parts. I could easily imagine how often they have sex during this passionate beginning of their relationship.

"Pleased to meet you, George," I smiled and said the same speech as I always did when Paula arrived to introduce us to each of her new the one and only.

Paula pulled me into a heartfelt "bear's embrace".

"You look like shit, sis," she shook her head disappointingly, viewing me as if she were a doctor looking at an ill patient. "Does it mean you can finally share the happy news with us?"

Sometimes, I hated Paula for her tasteless lack of empathy. She was well aware that we would share the happiness about my maternity with the family within seconds if the pregnancy test showed me those damn two stripes. Paula did everything to make me feel bad and rub it in that her life was much more successful than mine.

"Our life doesn't consist of as much news as yours," I said, smiling coldly and glanced at George in an obvious manner. Paula noticed it and quickly changed the subject.

"I'm starving," she announced and strode towards the kitchen without an invitation. "By the way, here, this is for the evening!" Paula beamed, and her eyelashes fluttered, praising her beautiful brown eyes as she handed me a bottle of wine.

I hoped that the dinner would pass calmly.

My sister knows that I'm not fond of red wine—I drink white wine only.

CHAPTER FIVE

The dinner was quite nice until Paula poured herself the third glass.

"Agri, I keep thinking—how do you take care of everything?" Paula pretended to be considerate, and I noticed how my husband glanced at her with great interest.

Meanwhile, George placed another slice of ham on his plate as if he hadn't had any food for weeks. I started doubting his giant torso was achieved by physical training and discipline.

"The company and its employees each has their own needs," Paula carried on with her loud theories, paying attention to my husband again. "Then, this house with all the effort you have put into it. Since our parents retired, they went to live in Riga and haven't done anything much here. But you did a flawless job with your own hands... The terrace is excellent, the pavement is perfect, and the lawn looks worthy of a manor in England. How do you find time for everything?"

"Thank you, Paula!" Agris grinned and placed his hand on top of mine unexpectedly. "Honestly, your sister takes care of the house, and she does brilliant work here."

I replied to my husband's gaze with a warm smile. Agris always defended me.

"By the way, Laura," Paula tried to do everything to irritate me, "aren't you going to return to work?"

"Currently, it's not in my plans," I growled and felt how Agris looked at me. I knew what he was thinking. Agris believes that I'm looking at things too negatively when it comes to my sister. He believes that Paula wishes nothing bad for me. He also knows something crucial about my sister, but he always pretends that this important thing has never happened.

Gladly, the doorbell rang unexpectedly, and it distracted Paula from poking her nose into my idle life.

"Perhaps your parents have arrived?" Agris suggested, squinting as always when he was surprised about something. Living in the countryside by a forest means that unexpected guests were a rarity.

"That's unlikely," I replied, standing up at the same time with my husband, but Agris was quicker to disappear towards the door.

Paula and George wasted no time, using the moment to touch each other under the table, convinced that I see nothing.

A moment later, Agris returned. "It's our neighbour. She's looking for you," he announced and sat down.

My eyes widened in surprise. It was past ten o'clock in the evening already. What would she want?

"Did you mean the woman from the other house?" I asked awkwardly.

"We have no other neighbours," Agris noted, and Paula lifted her chin attentively.

"Maybe we should invite her to join us?" my sister suggested.

"I don't know her that well." I stood up from the table and went towards the door.

She stood by the door on our porch, studying me with a deep and dramatical gaze. Under the artificial light, her hair dazzled with amber shades. Her strands were wet since getting to our house while it was sprinkling took a few minutes.

"Good evening, Laura!" she attempted to smile, although she sounded worried.

"Good evening," I replied, unable to hide my surprise for her visit at such a late hour. Was it even polite? Now I could look at the neighbour as arrogantly as she did a few days ago, but I saw no point in it. Perhaps something happened to her, and she needed help.

A moment later, I found out there was nothing wrong.

"I brought you some white wine," she handed me a bottle, and I grasped it, feeling perplexed. After examining the wine, I realised it wasn't the cheap type. Besides, she had nailed it—I only loved the white wine.

That reminded me of Paula's gift tonight, as it was the only bottle on the table, and my sister was the only one drinking from it. As always, she didn't care what to drink, so she got all the wine for herself. Agris rarely consumes any alcohol, but I would have had a glass. A couple of white wine glasses. Agris told me that I was exaggerating, thinking that Paula tried to irritate me on purpose, but I knew I was right. Paula does everything to remind me about THAT.

"Thank you," I replied, surprised. "Would you like to come in? We're having dinner." I opened the door a little wider.

"Oh, no, no, thank you," she gestured dismissively. "It's already late. I didn't want to disturb you this late, but I was restless the entire day about how I treated you earlier today. It was rude of me," she continued.

"Don't worry," I reassured, "It's okay. Besides, it happened days ago!"

She spared me a strange glance and said nothing. Once again, I felt odd. It was cold outside, and my neighbour stood by my house and eyed me.

"Enjoy your evening, Laura," after a moment, she glanced away and turned to leave. Confused, I kept standing there for a while, watching the vigorous wind rushes through Aya's hair. When my neighbour reached her house, she turned quickly to glance at me once again. Sadly, I couldn't see her expression from afar. Aya walked into her house and closed her door.

I returned to the others, and it seemed that two of them hadn't even noticed my absence. Paula kept telling Agris about her continuous success in the career path, and George eyed her with such admiration as if she were Jennifer Lopez's copy.

The following hour, Paula continued ignoring me and

kept sharing her travel adventures. I listened to her and couldn't stop thinking about where she found the time to merge her career and all four holidays within half a year. Yet, I decided to keep quiet. She only required the tiniest reason to pester me about my unemployment. The holiday discussions weren't trendy for me. Paula would probably say that every day is like a holiday for the unemployed. But she has no clue what it's like to be left without a job and feel useless.

While Paula, Agris and George shared their impressive adventures, I enjoyed my white wine until I noticed that the neighbour's bottle was nearly empty. I pretended to listen to my sister, silently thinking about my neighbour. Why did she come so late?

Moments before midnight, Paula and her lovebird finally decided to go home. I sighed in relief.

"It's late. Perhaps you'd like to stay over?" my husband suddenly offered. "The weather is terrible."

"Unfortunately, we must leave. George has a training tomorrow morning." Paula said sorrowfully. "But thanks for the offer, Agri!"

When they finally left, and my husband and I were left alone, Agris pulled me closer to him. It was a long kiss—a complete opposite to the storm that drummed outdoors.

"I'll take Dodger for a walk," he whispered apologetically. "The dog hasn't been outdoors today."

"It's wet and dark outside," I rushed to reply and added a joke, "During such weather, even dogs don't kick out their owners."

"Ten minutes, and we'll be back. I could do with some

fresh air, too," my husband explained. "Today was hell in the office."

"Has anything happened?" I asked. During our dinner, I noticed that Agris seemed concerned about something, only pretending to listen to our guests.

"It's okay. Some small issues," he put on a jacket and took Dodger's leash. "One of the clients is angry about a missing cargo. Nothing special."

"Nothing special?" My eyes widened in surprise. Of course, I understood very little about the logistics, but I knew that even delayed deliveries caused issues. The costs for a missing cargo could cost thousands.

"Will you be able to find it?" I was worried. "It can't just disappear."

"Darling, you shouldn't worry about it," Agris calmed me. "Dodger, come on, buddy!"

When Agris and Dodger left, I returned to the kitchen. I poured the rest of the wine into the sink because it felt like a drop more would remind me of the boredom. Perhaps I should talk to Agris—I could look for a job. Mom, most likely, was right that the baby will arrive on its own terms.

Nearly an hour had passed when I realised Agris hadn't returned home yet. I unlocked the door and stood there, listening to the silent noises. The street was empty, stretching into the darkness. The rain and wind raged, and I could hear thunder somewhere afar.

At first, I called my husband's name quietly, then louder until I started crying out, "Agri! Dodger! Agri!"

I didn't want to get changed into anything warmer.

Instead, I wrapped my arms around myself in the cold and went to have a look around the corner.

The sharp wind swayed the creepy tree branches, and the top of the forest trees painted strange signs as if trying to tell me something.

It was night. Nauseous anxiety took over me.

Agris didn't come home later either.

CHAPTER SIX

I blankly stared at the dark behind the kitchen window. Three hours had passed since Agris left the house. Panic took over my body. I put on a hoodie and went outside striding mechanically, unable to sit and wait, doing nothing. I locked the door, and after pacing in the empty garden, I went on the street. My neighbour's windows were dismissively dark. I decided to go down to the highway. The cold rain sprinkled over my face.

There were no surrounding noises anywhere near. Suddenly, panic and fear overwhelmed me. What if Agris had decided to have a walk down the highway and some car hit both—my husband and Dodger? No! I can't allow such horrible thoughts!

I was exhausted. Overwhelmed by despair, I stood on an empty road and begun to shed tears. The terrible gut feeling kept revisiting me. I wanted to howl like a dog. I started running, and the hood fell from off my head, my hair got wet, and the neat braid hit against my neck.

When I became breathless, I stopped for a moment. I was nearly by the highway. The queue of the twin houses looked like a scene from horror films—no lights, only a lonely, pitiful lantern shed a faint and insignificant dazzle. I glanced over my shoulder towards my house, hoping to see some light from the second-floor windows—maybe Agris had returned and lit the yellow light? No. It was only the outdoor lantern.

A moment later, I reached the highway. It seemed deserted. Strange. For the big roads, it was a rarity to be empty—even during nights.

"Agri!" I cried out into the damp air. I tried to listen to every sound—even the most insignificant ones—but nothing. It was a soundless desert. Finally, the devastation stepped away, and fury took its place. Anger at my husband's carelessness and his promise to come home within a few minutes—he hadn't fulfilled his promise.

Where could he be? I doubted he would go to the forest in the middle of the night.

Agris adored the woods. He took Dodger for short and long walks over there every evening. My husband had mentioned that his day at work wasn't successful. Something bothered him greatly. Maybe... Maybe he went to the forest after all? But at night? Oh, God, I have no clue why he would do that.

It was so foolish of him—promising me to return within ten minutes without taking his mobile phone, then disappear for hours in the darkness.

If Agris went to the forest, maybe he slipped over the wet leaves, fell over, pulled his leg, and Dodger could not help his owner. Agris must be waiting for help, but the night is too lonely, dark and foggy. We nearly live in complete isolation from the rest of the world—surrounded by woods and vacant lands.

While standing on the highway, a strange feeling took over me. The nightly wind caressed my forehead like a comforting, gentle hand. What was it? Did anyone truly touch me?

There was no point in letting the wind pull me apart, so I returned home. I didn't run anymore. Instead, I paced slowly, as if I were cursed. When I reached the yard, I glanced at my neighbour's windows. It seemed as if faint light gleamed in one of them. It could've been a nightlamp. A moment later, the light faded, and the darkness took over the area, the same as it took over my future life.

CHAPTER SEVEN

I woke up and realised that I was sleeping on the couch in the living room, rolled up like an embryo. I slid my gaze over the room. The tablecloth, spare dishes and the large juice pitcher was proof that the guests were really here yesterday—not only in my head. So the rest of the things that seared in my memory were true. I became breathless, and I sat up as my heartbeats started drumming. My father's clock on the wall showed that it was eight o'clock in the morning.

I rushed out of bed. My head was faintly spinning. But then, I came back to my senses.

It's morning, so Agris must have returned home, slept and should be upstairs. I made a fearful step forwards, gathered my courage and rushed upstairs. When I opened the bathroom door and peeked inside, there was nothing but emptiness. In the bedroom, there was only the neatly made bed from the day before. There were no signs that anyone had been in the room since the previous day. Not even in the kitchen, terrace or garage. Agris' car was parked in front of the garage, where he left it on arrival. I even looked inside the storage room, but only rows of toilet paper and household chemicals were stacked up neatly on the shelves. There was no sign of Dodger either. I had called for him countless times already. In the hallway, there was no Agri's jacket, no shoes, no Dodger's leash.

For a while, I remained standing at the open entrance door. I tried to breathe deeply to relieve any panic, but my fists started to clench. My dizziness faded, and the consciousness seemed to return. I gripped the door frame and glanced towards the forest. Maybe Agris is still there, but he can't get out of the woods without my help? Dodger is an intelligent pet—but also as old as the world—perhaps he's in trouble too? Wind could have ripped a heavy tree branch and pushed it on the pathway.

I closed my eyes, inhaled deeply and exhaled a hundred times fully. Then, I put on my sports shoes, a thicker jacket and filled my pockets with everything I could grab: my mobile phone, a camping knife—and for some reason—I even took a pack of tissues.

I was going to do it at some point. But only when I'd feel ready for it...

CHAPTER EIGHT

That day, I turned seven. Of course, every child is thrilled to have their birthdays. A few days ago, my father had returned from his first foreign business trip and brought my sister and me unusual packs of sweets and piles of small girly joys: lip glosses, bracelets, t-shirts, lace shorts, socks and colourful notebooks. But the birthday gift surpassed everything else. It was a small black handbag with pearly buttons, a braided belt and countless pockets inside. Perhaps it wasn't made of leather, but little girls didn't care about that. In any case, the material was high quality, the lining of the velvet inside was incredibly soft to the touch, the black pearls proudly displayed their round shapes. The handbag was truly worthy for a little princess. My happiness was impossible to express in words.

But Paula ruined everything. My sister was already ten—supposedly a big girl. But she threw a tantrum like a hysterical three-year-old.

When I unpacked the handbag, I examined every inch of

the little miracle in my hands, excited about the present. Paula stood next to me and remained silent with bitten lips. I placed the bag on my shoulder and proudly swayed in front of others, expecting some compliments. That moment, my sister started shrieking that I shouldn't have such a gift—that the handbag was should belong to her. Aunt Astrid—our dad's sister—grasped her head and quickly stood up from the table. It was the first time I heard the words "migraine", but the word disappeared somewhere between the shouting. Dad started yelling at Mom, blaming her for spoiling their daughters and saying it was all her fault. I went aside. Keeping my hand on my precious gift, I looked at my surroundings. Dad went outside to smoke. Aunt Astrid and Uncle Vilnus suddenly remembered that they had to go shopping as they kissed my cheeks in a rush, quickly moving towards the door. My mother escorted them to the exit and disappeared, probably in the kitchen. Only Paula remained in the living room, calmly sitting by the table in my seat and viewed me with a satisfied gaze. I couldn't tame my tears.

I had waited for my birthday so badly, but my sister ruined everything. Something struck me at that moment. I ran to Paula, and I grabbed her hair and smacked her surprised face with my free hand.

"You ruined everything!" I cried out. Paula screeched, demanding to let her go.

A second later, Mom ran to us. As soon as she saw what was happening, she started yelling.

"Laura, what are you doing? Let your sister go!"

"Mom, she slapped me!" Paula whined and started her

hysterical crying once again.

Dad opened the door, and as he noticed that nothing had changed, he added, "It's unnecessary. I will go to Riga. I'll be home very late." He slammed the door shut.

Dad always went away whenever we fought. Mom had once mentioned that he wanted a son because the scandals of the three women are driving him crazy.

"Laura! Paula! Calm down!" Mom was furious. "Laura, you can't hit your sister! As a punishment, I will take your handbag, and you won't see it for now."

I reminisced the feeling as if it happened yesterday. It was ironic—how little parents sometimes needed to say for the kids to remember it for the rest of their lives. My mother didn't mean to be spiteful, but the present she took away from me still hurts me. It wasn't just a handbag. It was parental love and attention. It was the feeling that finally, something beautiful belongs only to me and doesn't have to be shared with my sister. But it was taken away from me.

I ran away outside the house. Dad was away, and the backyard was empty. I went behind the corner of the house and strode towards the meadow. Mom shouted somewhere from behind, but I darted away so quickly as if I were chased. The tears poured down my cheeks too quickly for me to tame them.

First, I ran down the trail through the meadow and then down the path through the forest. Then, I bolted forwards until my legs no longer obeyed me, and I collapsed. It was the end of August, and my white sandals had gotten dirty with smashed blueberries, and sharp seeds of some plants were stuck on my dress. When I came back to my awareness, I was deep in the woods—so deep I couldn't find my way back.

I started panicking. I rushed to my feet to return home, but finding the road was impossible. I tried going down multiple trails, but strange spruces replaced the familiar pine trees, the tracks disappeared, and the forest drowned in the twilight, although it was daytime. I tried to find any foot trails, but they vanished between the footprints left by animals.

It took three days until anyone found me. Years later, I knew that the police had started searching for me on the first day, but it was in vain. I was found only in the evening on the third day. I was bitten by various bugs, starving and wet from the rain during the day before.

Sobbing and desperate, I had spent two nights in the forest, resting by a tree trunk and—more than anything else in the world—I wished for my parents to rescue me.

I was in all newspapers as the most sought child in Latvia. Some lady who had driven by the forest thought she saw the missing child on the highway, and it caused the policemen to suspect that I was a victim of some paedophile who could have lured me into a car.

They started searching for me in the woods only on the second day.

A young guard carried me out of the forest. Since that day, I have never stepped foot there. The fear never faded. It still held me in its claws.

CHAPTER NINE

Now I strode towards the forest confidently. I tried focusing on the dewy blossoms of the field docks on both sides of the trail. I attempted to look at the rowan bunches on the edge of the forest with a genuine gaze, trying to gather my courage and obstinacy. I can do this! My husband is probably here somewhere, and I must find him.

"Agri! Dodger!" I called out as loud as I could. No response.

The trail trickled deeper into the woods. Ordinary rowans, viburnum and hazels encompassed the area. It wasn't frightening yet. Walking further, I glanced over my shoulder a few times, ensuring that it was indeed only one trail. I wasn't a seven-year-old anymore, so everything should be okay this time. One careful step, then another—see, Laura, nothing terrible is happening.

Deeper in the woods, the bushes became thicker, and yesterday's rain made the wet leaves swoosh over my head, splashing large drops of water and a handful of yellow leaves from time to time. I continued walking. The silent forest unfolded before me, frozen windless.

As I glanced at my mobile phone, I concluded that an hour had passed since I left the house. There was no use to follow the animal trails any further—Agris wouldn't have gone that far. Nobody replied to the names I had called out a hundred times. Finally, I decided it was time to return home.

As I approached the house, I felt uneasy. The hope that my husband may be home sparked again. Maybe he's already sitting on the terrace, ready to explain to me what happened. But nobody was there on this side of the yard. The car stood exactly where it was parked. I locked the door behind me and walked around the house. Silence. Nobody around. I saw Agris' phone on the desk in the hallway. All this time, it had safely lain there. I was so worried that I hadn't even thought of calling him during the night.

I grabbed the phone and tried to turn it on, but it was discharged. The charger had to be somewhere near. I thought the last time I saw it was in the bedroom. I rushed upstairs and searched all Agris' drawers. Strange, but they were empty, and the charger was nowhere. I decided that my husband might have forgotten in at the office.

I wanted to clear my head or at least have a cup of coffee. I turned on the kettle and put Agris' phone near, thinking about what to do next. It would take fifteen minutes to drive to Tukums police station. I should go there and write a report about my husband's disappearance. It was almost noon, and I had no reason to wait any longer.

I felt more lively after the craved coffee. I checked if my

passport and walled were in the bag, and I put on an autumn coat to go to the police station when I suddenly remembered to take Agris phone. Suddenly, I realised—I should take his SIM card and put it in my own phone. Perhaps I could guess his password. Maybe he called anyone before leaving the house, and that would explain where he went.

I opened his phone. But there was no SIM card.

As usual, the car key lay on the shelf at the entrance doors. I got in the car, glanced at the back for a moment. The car was clean—Agris' belongings weren't there, not even inside the glove shelf. I concluded that he had recently cleaned the vehicle. We often argued about it. Agris car was always like a home on wheels with everything you may need: starting with mineral water bottles and energy bar stocks, ending with socks that hadn't found their way home. Mess in the car was one of my husband's rare shortcomings.

The small side streets of Tukums were empty on Saturday morning, and the only activities were on the local market square. A young duty officer sat by a window of the run-down police station. He looked like a youngster with a gloomy face and sunken facial features.

"Good afternoon!" I addressed the police station's duty officer. My voice felt hoarse and agitated. "A man has gone missing. I need help."

The station was quite dark. I saw only a couple of employees behind the on-call post, but none of them turned their heads towards me. But the young long-faced policemen looked at me carefully.

"What happened to you?" he asked in a calm voice.

"My husband is missing," I said hurriedly. "At night, he went for a short walk with our dog, and he hasn't returned home yet.

"Did he have a phone with him? Did you try calling him?"

"He left his phone at home," I replied. "He didn't take it with him."

"Perhaps he met an acquaintance and—" the policeman offered a version, but I stopped him halfheartedly.

"No, it's not an option. We live in a private house in a rural area with only one neighbour and a forest nearby. And my husband doesn't know our neighbour. Last night, he arrived home after eight o'clock. We had guests—my sister and her partner. After their departure, my husband said he would go for a short walking with our dog. It should have been just ten minutes." I could no longer sustain the flood of tears streaming from my cheeks. Finally, I started crying out loud, and the cop handed me a paper tissue expressionlessly.

"Calm down, come in here."

I was invited into a pale grey room with only one grey computer desk and a couple of chairs. I remained on my feet, unable to calm down.

Now, another employee was talking to me—a few years older, calmer and much more understanding.

"Missing men usually return home relatively quickly, but I will not stop you from writing the report."

I sat down and wiped my eyes.

"Shall we begin?" the policeman asked, glancing at me.

It seemed that he had noticed my panic and realised that

I wouldn't leave until I get some help to find Agris.

"Yes. Please help me find him...."

"When was the last time you saw your husband?" he asked, typing everything on the computer. "What's his name, surname, age."

"At night, he went for a walk with our dog Dodger. It was after midnight," I explained again. "My husband's name is Agris Redlich. He's thirty-five years old. We've been married for almost six months.

"Did your husband say when he would come home? Maybe he planned to go somewhere else?" The policeman turned to me, lifting his chin.

"He only went for a short walk! At night. He should have returned within ten minutes!" I shouted and quickly recollected myself.

The policeman pretended not to hear my harsh reaction and continued the interrogation, "And the dog hasn't returned home either?"

"No. He's gone, too."

"Did your husband have any drinking problems? Could it be possible that he went out to grab a drink?"

"Absolutely not!" I rushed the words. "My husband would rarely have a beer—truly rarely. He doesn't even smoke."

Was it my imagination, or did the policeman's expression change? It seemed as if he disliked what I'd said.

He remained silent for a tiny moment. Then, the questions poured with a new wave. "You've mentioned that you live in a rural area. Where exactly?" he asked.

"We live in Pures district, not far from the highway. The Woodwalks."

Another strange grimace flared up in the man's face.

"I'll find out if there are any reports about any car accidents in your area. Also, it's crucial to find out who your husband has contacted in the past few days: who he has spoken to, met or seen."

"I went to the highway during the night. There were no accidents."

"Did your husband have any issues at work? Maybe he seemed distressed?" the policeman continued questioning me.

I wasn't sure what to reply. Yes, my husband was a little concerned when he arrived home. I recalled how Agris had appeared to be preoccupied with his thoughts during the dinner. Maybe it was related to the lost cargo?

"Indeed, he seemed a little distressed for a moment," I confessed. "He said their company had lost some freight. My husband manages logistics."

The policeman's face was handsome, but his breath smelled of cigarettes. But now, he was my only hope. This inspector had to find my husband. He moved his fingers slowly over the keyboard to record my statement, and the poor speed irritated me. Even when he raised his head, he did it with a precise but phlegmatic movement. Any second could turn out crucial for my husband, but this man moved like a river after trickling into the sea. The idea that Agris was still in the forest—gotten into an accident or stuck in a swamp—made me restless. What if he ad Dodger got attacked by a wild animal? There were plenty of stories about wild boars attacking people in the woods, but that usually happened only when they had their piglets—in October.

When I told the policeman all about it—the forest, animals and swamps—he was unable to mask his disbelief.

"I know that forest. Yes, the woods are thick, but the place is no more than seventeen acres. A grown-up can't get lost there, and the animals won't attack to defend their families during this season. Only a child can get lost there," the inspector faltered, saying the last words. His gaze lowered to his palms before the man tried to continue the conversation quickly and suggested to check when was the last time my husband was seen on social media.

I shook my head dismissively. "My husband uses only his e-mail. He's not registered on any social media platforms as he finds them obnoxious."

"It's rare nowadays." The policeman seemed shocked. "Try to ensure that your husband hasn't gone to visit his parents, relatives, friends or colleagues. We will contact the ambulance, local hospitals and the morgue."

"My husband's parents are dead. I'll call my husband's office when I get home. I don't have the number with me."

"Is that so? Do you have a new phone that doesn't include any of the old contact numbers?" the man asked, but I failed to understand what he meant.

"In our family, we don't disturb each other during the working hours. I have written down his office number somewhere."

"Well then, you're free to go home and wait," the policeman said and returned my passport after taking my details, "I will contact you today."

I went outside the police station and realised it was nearly lunchtime when I inhaled the fresh air. Standing by the autumn flower beds, images from my childhood surged to my memory. Back then, when I'd heard someone calling my name, I realised there was hope. I yelled back, but my voice was nothing more than a birds cry. Crawling out from under the pine trees, I called out once more—more successfully this time because I had managed to gather all my strength. And then, I noticed some sudden movement. Something flashed on the right side; something green, green-brown behind the small pine. Then, a young man appeared, dressed in a military uniform. I could still remember him as if it were yesterday—the way he had leaned in as soon as he noticed me, reassuring me that I have nothing to fear, promising he would take me to my mom and dad. He approached me slowly—hands stretched—until he could reach my shoulder. The man knelt down, smiled and embraced me. He was the most handsome grown-up man I had ever seen. He didn't seem as old as my dad and reminded me of Aunt Astrid's twenty-year-old son.

Then, he picked me up and carried me. On our way out of the woods, he took a walkie-talkie, reporting that he had found the girl on the northeast. Yes, even now, I still remember—northeast. The rest of it, however, is blurred. We went to a meadow by the forest—bathed in twilight—and that's when I noticed my parents. A crowd of people surrounded them, rushing towards us all at once. But I was baffled to see my dad cry. Everyone cried—my mom and even those other people. Even Paula, who held out mother's hand tightly—as if trying to hold back the urge to run to me.

I noticed that there were other people in the meadow, too. Soon, the crowd surrounded us. Some of the strangers tried to take photos of me in my father's embrace, but the military man hid my face under his jacket that he had given me while we strolled through the woods. It allowed me to hide from all those eyes and look at Paula in safety. I urged to know—was my sister crying because I was in the centre of attention, or did she genuinely worry about me?

I've never dared to ask her about it. Not when I was seven, seventeen, nor thirty-two years old.

CHAPTER TEN

When I left the police station, the autumn breeze laughed in the air, and gloomy clouds surrounded the sky. Fifteen hours have passed since Agris left home. A loud pulse rustled in my head, and I felt as if I was having the worst hangover in the world. I sat in my car and decided I won't wait a moment longer. I'll call Agris's office and do everything I can to ensure he's come home.

I didn't have Vintors Cargo Transportation phone number on my phone, but I quickly googled the company.

You must do this, Laura!

My eyes were bloodshot from crying. I was desperate to talk to someone, get a piece of advice or some support. First, I decided to call Paula, but her phone was switched off. It was no surprise—it was always hard to get in touch with her, but right now—I need her more than I've ever had. Paula had met Agris yesterday. She left our house only a few moments before my husband disappeared. Maybe she's seen something. Perhaps Agris has told her something important, a clue like in the detective movies or novels.

My head began to ache excruciatingly, and something flickered before my eyes. It was probably a migraine—the sharp headache that seems to torture me on a regular basis. I found my medicines in the handbag and popped two in my mouth without hesitation. I had no water, so swallowing them was a challenge, although the pills were tiny.

A moment later, I felt a little better, so I called my husband's office. I sat in my car motionless, my heart drumming ferally. Only a few seconds later, somebody replied to my call.

"Vintors Cargo Transportation, how can I help?" a kind female voice replied confidently. I wondered who she was. I had never visited Agris at work, and I know very little about his colleagues and friends at work, to be honest. He's simply one of those people who doesn't bring his work home—Agris once said it himself. Now that my husband had gone missing, I sat in the car trying to tame my trembling fingers, and I suddenly realised that I knew nothing about his job. I was aware only of the fact that he's dealing with cargo transportations, and they sometimes go missing because somebody steals them, the drivers occasionally lie, the clients can get impatient wanting to get their delivery as soon as possible—but that's about it. That's all I know. Nothing else.

"Hello. My name is Laura Redlich. I'm Agris Redlich's wife. Could you please tell me if he's come to work today? I can't get in touch with him this morning, but it's incredibly urgent," I rushed my words as quickly as I could.

Silence. Odd stillness on the other side.

"Hello? Can you hear me?" I repeated.

"Yes... but... I'm sorry, but we don't have anyone named Agris working here," the woman's gentle voice sounded somehow distant, but my heart started screaming with wild beats.

"I'm talking to Vintors Cargo Transportation LTD, is that right? In Riga?"

"Yes, that's correct," the woman said.

"And you're saying Agris Redlich doesn't work there? The director of the logistics—Agris Redlich?" I wiped my sweaty hair away from my face, trying to speak calmly.

"No, unfortunately, not. Perhaps you've called the wrong number. Our managing director's name is Karlis Bankovskis," she replied before the signal got cut.

Did she just drop the call on me? Impossible. Nobody would do that.

I tried to call again, but it was no use—there were only silent beeps. Mortified, I sat in my car, unable to make a sound.

Once, when Agris had gone to work, and I remained lonely at home, a bitter thought crossed my mind—what if marriage union of two people doesn't even exist? Every soul lives its own journey, and its core is an enigma. And although you think you know your partner incredibly well, sometimes you still feel like beating your head against a wall or falling into some pit.

Suddenly, I realised that, perhaps, I didn't know my husband well enough.

During the evening, I wasn't brave nor strong, and the headache had returned. I lay down on the sofa in the living room, holding a cold, wet cloth on my forehead, when a sudden sound of a driving car startled me. I jolted to my feet and ran to the window. A police car had parked in front of the house, and a man in a uniform left the car. It was the same policeman who had taken my report earlier during the day. I stepped onto the porch. The man approached me, his eyes low. I was petrified, wishing I could stop the time.

We've found your husband. I'm very sorry.

I feared those words. He wasn't allowed to say them. Those words would kill me for sure.

"Good evening, Laura," he greeted me with a handshake. I replied to it with a limp and trembling hand.

"Have you found my husband?"

"I forgot to introduce myself earlier today. My name is Richard Vitols, the chief inspector of Tukums," he reported.

I couldn't care less about his name, and he could probably read it in my eyes, so he started talking a little faster.

"May I come in?"

I gestured towards the open door and escorted the inspector to the living room. A moment later, Mr Vitols sat on a chair, examining my face deeply, making me look away.

Talk! Now! Don't make me wait any longer!

"Please, say something," I begged.

"Laura, we checked all of the information you've provided and spoke to a few people," the man announced loud and clear, but I still felt like his words were too slow. "Unfortunately, your report has been declined."

"What?" I smiled, bemused and disbelieving his words.

The inspector cleared his throat. "Laura, you're not married. You don't have a husband."

Silence stretched for a few seconds before mad laughter escaped my lips.

"Of course, I've heard that police does everything to avoid a case, but I never expected anything like this!"

"I'm very sorry, Laura," he continued the awful joke. "If

you need psychological assistance, here are some contacts of municipal specialists."

He handed me a grey business card, but I stood frozen, unable to move.

Agris! This is a stupid joke!

"Has Agris arranged this joke?" I started laughing hysterically. "Agri? Come here, did you hear this?" I rushed to my feet, looking outside the window, assuming that Agris had arrived with the policeman to fool me.

"Of course, it's not my business, but perhaps you should move to a city?" Richard Vitols changed the subject as if the previous conversation was unimportant. "You're a young woman, living in complete isolation. Sometimes it's too much to bear."

"Are you insane? I'm not living on my own!" My patience dissipated. If it could be measured in drops, this was the last one. "Is this my husband's stupid idea of a joke?" I continued, "Look at this ring!" I demonstrated my wedding ring. "Look around, see the garden and the garage! We live here together—my husband Agris Redlich and I, and our dog!" I screamed.

The policeman glanced around the room where most of my husband's belongings were.

A second later, he asked, "Laura, you don't have an officially registered marriage. We were unable to find any living man named Agris Redlich in our records. The workplace you mentioned indeed exists, but nobody there knew this man's name when we called them."

I froze. I stood there, my arms crossed, lips tight, and a volcano ready to erupt where my heart was, threatening to trickle through my veins like flames.

"Your jokes are idiotic," I gasped, unable to speak after what I'd heard.

The inspector became quiet. Instead, he opened his folder, took out a few papers and handed them to me.

"As I already said, Laura, the man you've reported doesn't live in Latvia at the moment. We can't open the case to look for him."

"Go to hell!" I yelled, gesturing towards the door. "Get the hell out of my house! I'll write a complaint about your incompetence tomorrow. I'll sue the entire damned office!"

The inspector kept eyeing me with his brown eyes calmly. He was about to head out when he turned to face me once more.

"Could you show me any of your husband's belongings?" he suddenly asked.

I grasped the wall behind me, disbelieving that I was participating in this farce.

"Are you mocking me?" I hissed.

"Not at all, Laura," he replied calmly. "I'm only trying to give you a chance."

His peaceful face made me want to puke. I turned quickly, inviting the man to follow me.

"Will a marriage certificate do?" I asked as we headed upstairs. The policeman followed me. "Agris Relich's clothing? Personal belongings? I have everything you could imagine."

When we entered the bedroom, it looked incredibly cosy. The light birch furniture gave the room cleanliness and a splendour atmosphere. A bouquet of beige asters sat in the white porcelain vase on my bedside table. Agris's bedside table was empty. He doesn't like flowers.

With a rough jolt, I swung the wardrobe open. I froze motionlessly. Had Agris moved his clothes to the drawers? Impossible! He couldn't hang a suit in the drawers. Only my dresses, blouses and skirts hung in the wardrobe.

I turned my head, trying to avoid the inspector's eye contact because I knew he was waiting for my reaction.

"Agris is a minimalist," I muttered. "He doesn't require too many things. But I'll show you our photographs and documents."

Did I sound crazy? Most likely.

We went back downstairs and went to my husband's office next to the living room. He'd occasionally work there from home.

My knees turned numb and wobbly before I managed to step into the room. It was almost empty. There was only a table covered in a white tablecloth. The office was dusty, as if nobody had stepped a foot here for months.

This must be another one of my nightmares.

A terrifying, vile, disgusting nightmare.

This would never happen in real life.

It's impossible in real life; it's not a TV show.

"I believe it's time for me to go," the inspector said, standing right behind me. "I'd be really happy if you try visiting a psychologist. They are good people. They will help you."

I turned around.

"Do you really think I've lost my mind and my husband is just a fruit of my imagination?" I shrieked so vigorously that it shot my saliva at his face. "The man is missing, and you're trying to refer me to a psychologist?"

"Laura..." he wiped his face thoroughly and took a step

towards me. "Protecting the citizens is my duty, not hurting them. The police can't step into this if there's no trace of crime or a real missing person. We can't look for somebody who doesn't exist."

"Is that so? Doesn't exist? Absurd! Absurd! Absurd!" I shouted, throwing my arms up, but the man no longer listened to me. He headed towards the door. When he was by the exit, I asked him to stop once more.

"Please," I said, "Let's go to my neighbour. She lives nearby. She will tell you I don't live on my own."

"The inspector shook his head and added in a wise voice, "Miss, I must return to work. Besides, your neighbour may not be home."

By now, I was convinced the man thought I was insane. This time, I recollected my composure.

"Only five minutes. Please..."

"Fine. If it means so much to you, let's go," he sighed heavily and allowed me to lead the way.

CHAPTER ELEVEN

We reached my neighbour's yard, and I could see from afar that she was home. Her Passat was parked by the house, and her shadow dashed past the kitchen window.

Slightly opening the door, Aya took a step backwards.

"Police?" she gasped, lifting her eyebrows in surprise and viewing me apprehensively. "How can I help you?"

"Aya!" I spoke immediately before the inspector would. "I can't find the words to explain the nonsense happening right now, but could you tell this officer that I live with my husband—Agris—and that we own a labrador retriever, please?" I smiled to make this circus seem as harmless as possible. Yet, I couldn't deny my embarrassment for this absurd situation.

Rihards Vitols looked tired, but he said nothing about it. Instead, he patiently waited for Aya's reaction.

My neighbour's facial expression changed. She eyed me, then the police officer, odd nervousness gleaming in her gaze.

For God's sake, are you really that dumb? Just tell him

your neighbours are a married couple with a dog and that's all!

"I'm sorry, Laura, but I won't be able to help here," she glanced at me like I was some disaster.

"Your neighbour claims her husband has gone missing. We're trying to help her, which is why we came to see you. Do you know Agris Redlich?" the inspector joined the discussion.

"I'm sorry to hear that. But no, I don't know this man. I'm afraid I can't help," Aya replied, continuing to eye me suspiciously.

Are they actors of a theatre? Is this a movie scene where I'm forced to film against my will?

"You know my husband! We invited you to join us when we had guests last night! You even gave me a bottle of white wine. Agris opened the door for you when you arrived at our porch yesterday!

Aya remained silent, continuing to stare at me with strange dark eyes. Suddenly, she faltered, talking to me, not the police officer, "Laura! Since the moment I live here, I haven't noticed that you'd live with anyone else. You live here alone. I haven't seen a dog, nor a cat. Yesterday, I did visit you," Aya added confidently. "I brought you wine to thank you for the pie you had given me. That's all."

"Thank you for your time," Officer Richard clearly seemed eager to end the conversation.

I glanced at Aya, then at the inspector. I had a feeling they were hiding something from me. Perhaps they knew each other.

"I don't know what's going on here, but I'll find it out," I forced the words over my lips.

"If there's any way I can help, I'm always happy to assist," Aya continued to act as if she didn't know me. I tried to look into her eyes, but the neighbour avoided my gaze. I had no doubts she purposely offered her false help. She just wanted to get rid of me.

"Good night," Richard Vitols thanked her, glanced at me and headed back to my house.

I had no choice but to follow him. I left Aya's yard, feeling breathless from the amount of anger. Then, I realised I hadn't heard my neighbour shut the door behind her. I turned around quickly. She stood on the porch, still eyeing me.

"Aya?"

"Yes?" she replied and nervously looked away immediately.

"You lied. But why?" I asked.

The neighbour sighed and slammed the door shut. I could hear the key turn twice.

The inspector didn't discuss the issue any further. Instead, he made excuses about having to leave.

That night, I spent a long while sitting in the kitchen in the dark. The last of the three light bulbs had burnt out. I sincerely wanted Agris to come home, find the box with spare light bulbs, and ensure we have bright lights that embrace every corner with a sense of safety.

Nothing would ever be the same. And it frightened me.

CHAPTER TWELVE

The large living room was cold in the frigid evenings. There was no firewood in the fireplace, but I was able to turn on the electric hearth. Its chaotic lights looked joyful, and they cheered me up a little. I sat on the wide windowsill, my elbows pressed resting on my knees, my palms holding my chin as I watched the flames dance.

The time dissipated. I heard a car door slam outside. I hadn't noticed how Dad's Volvo had appeared by the house. Finally, somebody arrived to support. Some day, all of us will laugh at this ridiculous situation. Perhaps I'll say it was an awfully realistic nightmare. We will sit by the round table with a brocade tablecloth that Mom once gave me. Possibly there will be a snowstorm behind the window, Agris will have carried some firewood inside, Dodger will make the lobby dirty with his paws, and Mom will rush to clean up the mess. My husband will be listening to my stories about the nightmares of his disappearance. My parents will smile. Perhaps only Paula would throw a mean phrase.

Mom and Dad entered the house without knocking since the door was left unlocked. I could hear them remove their jackets in the lobby, but I sat where I was, waiting patiently.

My mother is a shy woman with pale blue eyes and a pleasant voice. She's always been slender and held her head high. It was almost unbelievable that a baker could keep herself in such good shape. My father, on the other hand, is tall with a massive physique, an expressive face with thick eyebrows and dark eyes, and he has no signs of grey in his thick hair.

Both entered the kitchen, and only a candle awaited for them. Perhaps they brought some food, I thought. Then, Dad called for me. I wanted to respond loudly, but I managed only a faint whisper. Maybe I've caught a cold. As soon as my parents heard my whispers, they came to me.

Dad caressed my shoulder, and I began sobbing.

"Thanks for coming," I slid into Dad's warm caress and remained where I was. "I couldn't get in touch with Paula."

"It's all right, dear," Dad replied softly. "Parents are meant to support their children whenever they need it. Don't worry about Paula. She called us earlier and warned that she would have a busy meeting at work."

Mom kissed my cheek and went to the kitchen. She returned with a tray full of snacks and tea and sat by my side a moment later.

"Child, you look awful," she examined me from head to toe. "Climb down that windowsill. Tell me, what happened?"

I moved to the armchair and took the cup of tea that Mom had prepared.

"Something horrible has happened," I gasped.

"Darling, what's going on? You called us, but it was difficult to understand what happened."

"Agris has gone missing," I sobbed. My voice shook, "Yesterday, Paula and her new boyfriend came to visit us. They left after midnight. Agris went for a walk with Dodger. He said he'd be gone only ten minutes, but they never came home. I don't know what to do. Police declined to look into it. They acted..." I talked and talked, unable to stop until I glanced at my parents. Then, I froze. The words refused to leave my mouth.

My mother's eyes were full of worries, but my father sulked, grasping his forehead grimly. I went silent.

Finally, somebody broke the silence.

"Darling, who's Agris?" Dad asked, his voice stern. "Do you have a new boyfriend that we don't know about?"

Cold shivers took over my bones; they began somewhere deep in my core and spread across my entire body. A loud pulse drummed in my ears, and everything dissolved before my eyes.

CHAPTER THIRTEEN

I opened my eyes. I was sleeping on a couch in the living room, and a stranger stood by my side. The man's hair was concise, and he had crystal clear glasses with a golden frame. I'm not sure why, but he wore pale blue trousers and a jacket that I had seen somewhere before.

"Laura! Can you hear me?" he asked, examining me. I tried to understand why strangers were in my house. My parents stood by the door and spoke to some lady, but I couldn't see her face. She wore a blue jacket with red and white embroideries. Only then I realised – it was the ambulance uniform.

"What happened?" I asked, trying to sit up, but the unfamiliar man held me.

"Lay down. You fainted, and your parents called the ambulance. We've injected a mild sedative to calm you. It will be best if you remain in bed for a while. Your blood pressure is all right. When possible, it would be best if you see your GP."

Mom left the woman she spoke to and came to me.

"Laura, please listen to the doctors," she begged. "You collapsed. We had to call the doctors."

I didn't reply. I was powerless and unable to move.

"I'll walk you to the door." Dad escorted the medical crew to the exit.

Mom sat down on the edge of the sofa.

"You said you were dizzy, and then you collapsed on the floor," she explained. "Have some sleep. Afterwards, we must have a serious talk."

"I wanted to tell you the same thing," I tried to sound harsh, but I failed. My voice came out unexpectedly frail.

When Dad returned, he looked distressed. I know—he gets upset quite quickly.

"Laura, what's going on?" he tried to appear calm, but his stern voice made him sound demanding.

"Don't raise your voice," Mom requested. "The doctor said she needs some rest."

"Your mother has a poor heart condition, and you make this circus!" Dad seemed furious.

"All of you are insane!" I emphasised. "Agris has gone missing! Yet, instead of going to look for him, you decided to drug me!"

"Darling, we don't know anyone named Agris," Mom repeated the frightening words.

"I told you that giving her this house was a foolish idea," Dad growled. "Living here alone has probably made her consume alcohol and caused overactive fantasies!"

"Please, let your daughter speak, will you?" Mom hissed.

Then, she grasped my hand.

"So, even you think I'm not married?" I managed to ask calmly, although I had to admit—the previous night and this day had shattered my daily life, and I was no longer sure what to believe.

"Well, your mother and I weren't invited to any wedding!" Dad glanced at the ceiling, irritated.

"Dear," Mom petted my palm, gazing into my eyes worriedly. "The doctors said you might be feeling ill because of the hangover. Please, tell us the truth. Have you started drinking? We found empty wine bottles in the kitchen."

"All of you are crazy!" I pushed my head deeper into the pillow and angrily growled. "I can't drink. At least, not a lot!"

I kept getting sleepier. At this point, I started hating my parents.

"Laura, it was your choice to stay here and live on your own. Besides... Sooner or later, a man would come to live here with you," Mom continued talking some nonsense. "You lost your job. Now, it's visible how much it has shattered you. We feel guilty that we didn't come to visit you more often. We thought it would be for the best."

"I'm not alone," I replied. "I have a husband and a dog."

"Laura, please, don't frighten me," suddenly, Mom began to cry. Dad spared me a glance and started to pace by the window, nervously looking outside.

"Mara, calm down!" Dad yelled at my mother. "She's only saying those things under the influence of drugs or alcohol. You saw those bottles of wine in the kitchen. I'll call a doctor I know quite well. Perhaps we'll have to take her to a hospital."

"I'm not going anywhere," I hid my face under a blanket.

Such discussions made my exhaustion retreat. I quivered, feeling apprehension and anger rising within me. I had something to tell both of them. Rigorously, I threw the blanket off. Why wouldn't I tell them everything right now?

"I don't seem to sense any guilt here! You allowed your child to spend three days and nights in a forest alone, letting your kid survive on blueberries and dew! I could've had eaten poisonous berries and died suffering there! I'll call Paula now, and she will tell you everything. She was here with her boyfriend last night. It was Paula who drunk that red wine. And my husband—he sat there by the table with us."

My parents glanced at me, looking bewildered.

"Then call here," Dad continued. "Paula should have told you the truth a long time ago. Your mother and I have never supported the things she does."

"What are you talking about?"

"Call her," Dad handed me his phone with Paula's number already dialled on the screen. "Your sister must put an end to it at once."

"Maybe not now?" Mom tried to take the mobile from my hands, but I wouldn't let her.

"Mara! Hell! This has to end!" Dad growled.

"Do you want our daughter to go to a madhouse?"

While my parents argued, I waited for Paula to answer my call.

"Paula," I pronounced my sister's name slowly. "I have no clue what's going on, but if you know anything and care for me at all, please tell me the truth."

There was no quick response—only a heavy sigh.

"Laura, I'm sorry!" Paula muttered. "I didn't want to tell you this over the phone... But our parents called me and told me how poorly you seem. You collapsed. So I don't have a choice."

"Paula? What are you talking about? Do you know where my husband is?"

"You don't have a husband!" Paula confessed. "Agris doesn't exist. Sometimes, you mentioned him. At first, I thought you have a boyfriend which I haven't met yet. But eventually, I realised there is no Agris. You looked so devastated after losing your job, so I didn't want to hurt you. I thought—if I played along, you'd feel better. Now I know I shouldn't have done that."

"Were you here last night?" I asked calmly.

"Yes," Paula halted, reconsidering her every word. "I was there with George, my new boyfriend. You acted completely normal. You laughed. We talked about travelling and my job."

"And Agris wasn't sitting with us?"

"Laura, listen, I'm sorry. No, he wasn't." Paula said. "You've never introduced me to your boyfriend."

"Weren't you talking to Agris yesterday? Didn't you tell him how well he'd managed to take care of our house? You complimented the terrace and the lawn! Paula, you know Agris very well! You know him better than I do!"

"No, Laura, no," she replied after a moment of silence. "George and I visited you, and you were alone. I wanted to stay over, but you didn't want that. So we left."

I got angry.

"I don't want to see you ever again! Do you hear me? You're a liar, Paula! All of you are liars!" I yelled to ensure everyone heard me.

Dad ripped the phone from my hands and grasped me tightly, trying to calm me. I limped helplessly in his arms. Through his armpit, I watched the electric fireplace sparkle with flames. Dad, Mom, Paula and even the flame— everything was artificial here; unreal.

I felt like I had lost my mind, and my husband was only an imaginary silhouette. He wasn't real. Nothing was real.

CHAPTER FOURTEEN

A week later

"How bad is it?" I heard Paula's voice from the first floor. They didn't suspect I was already up and stood by the stairs on the second floor. Paula had just arrived and stood in the living room in her coat, quietly talking to our parents.

"The past few days have been better," Mom sighed heavily. Dad stood by her side and nodded. "She doesn't talk about the imaginary man and has begun eating a little. The first week was hard.

"It doesn't change the fact that she requires a psychiatrist's help," Dad added.

Paula hung her coat and headed to the kitchen. I had to take a few steps down the stairs to hear their conversation.

"I agree," Paula said. "Mom, this can't continue. She's not normal! She's imagined herself a husband! Don't you see it? It's a severe condition—perhaps even schizophrenia!

"Stop it, Paula!" Mom objected. "I spoke to the doctor. He said that the imagination could take fantasy for reality when a person experiences significant amounts of stress. It must be because she lost her job. She's just more upset than we realised. But it can all be cured at home—with pills and a mindful lifestyle. That's why we're by Laura's side. Later, when we must sell this house, we'll help her find a new job, and she can live with us. Letting her live here on her own wasn't the right thing to do.

"I agree," Paula admitted. "If I lived here—in the forsaken countryside—I'd probably lose my marbles, too.

"Actually, little miss, you grew up here," Dad reminded.

"Yes, but that was my childhood, and it was nice here," Paula continued. "Now look outside—the grass is long enough to reach your armpits."

Holding on to the stairwell, I stumbled back to my bedroom. I felt fragile. Most likely, I had lost a lot of weight. Fatigue surrounded every inch of my body, and my headache led me to despair.

In my bedroom, I stopped by the window and carefully glanced outside. Yes... the grass was so tall it started leaning sideways in some places. It probably grew all summer long—that's how high it was. Dry pieces of bark lay around the bare ash trees.

So, was it true? Had I really lost my mind and imagined my husband? In reality, I was just a maiden who lost her job and lives in a lonely, run-down house by a forest. Agris hasn't mowed the lawn since he doesn't exist. But of course, the empty wardrobe, the mobile phone with no SIM card... but what about Dodger?

Perhaps my sister's right, and I need serious therapy.

Somebody entered my bedroom. Mom called for me, but I didn't even bother looking back at her. I continued staring outside the dirty window, pondering how to accept my madness. How long have I been insane? A few weeks? Months? I have no clue what date it is today, what day of the week.

"Darling, are you up already?" Mom spoke tenderly, coming closer.

"As you can see," I replied coldly. "I want to be alone. I think it's time for you to return to Riga."

"What are you talking about?" Mom objected.

"I don't want to hear anything, Mom!" I groaned and turned to face her.

She's concerned about me, that was not deniable, but I must deal with the mess in my head on my own. "I agree to visit a psychiatrist, I assure you. I'll take care of it.

"You need your family," Mom protested.

"No, Mom, what I need is peace. You keep discussing my psychological state, and I can't stand it anymore! Besides, this house belongs to me now. Mom, I'm thirty-two. You can't make decisions about selling my house."

"Laura! Nowadays, people your age don't live such solitary life in isolation," Paula appeared behind Mom's back.

"You, Paula, better shut up!" I growled. "I don't care about the social stereotypes! I love this place."

"In Riga, we will be near you," Dad showed up.

"You all can go to Riga! I hate Riga! And I hate you, too!

I promise to visit a psychiatrist. But if you don't leave me now, I swear I'll kill myself!"

"Okay, okay, dear, just calm down," Mom and Dad glanced at each other, and I realised I had achieved my goal.

"But you must promise to keep your phone near and that you'll let us visit you soon, okay?" Paula murmured.

"Deal," I agreed, although I didn't want to see anyone. But when necessary, I can be crafty.

I truly wanted only one thing—for Agris to return home. I wished to wake up from the nightmare.

But my eyes were already open.

CHAPTER FIFTEEN

When my parents and sister departed, I wrapped myself in a blanket and slept for a couple of hours. Sleep helped me to stop thinking about the events I was unable to explain. I got up in the evening. Despite the late hour, I made myself a cup of strong coffee and two enormous sandwiches to ease the nauseating hunger. I enjoyed the feeling of solitude—nobody tried to irritate or lecture me. I went into the bathroom and glanced around. The last time I was here was a week ago. I opened the door to my husband's office, but there was no proof that a man had lived here. Go wherever you like—but only empty rooms, dusty corners and loneliness unveiled before my eyes.

I was unable to find any of my husband's belongings. I had searched every corner, even the storage room, but I found only spider webs.

Paula said that the ring on my finger wasn't a wedding ring. Yes, I remember now—my parents had given it to me after I graduated, and I wore it on my fourth finger.

Agris is only a fruit of my imagination—that's what everyone said, and I started believing them. I had created my own little world, ruled by endless fantasy.

"You were shattered when you lost your job," my parents' voices still echoed in my ears.

I adored that job. I got fired. Unable to get over it, I invented an imaginary family for myself.

I don't have any photos of Agris. I only have a bunch of absurd memories that cannot be explained. But I want to know one thing—if I truly lost my mind after getting fired, and my loneliness made up an imaginary husband—why do my memories feel so real? Why?

I got thirsty. I wanted to have a drink from the tap in the kitchen. But I forced myself to make a cup of light tea. Gloomy droplets of rain ran down the window again. Was it never going to stop? The weather was more depressing than my life. I opened the kitchen window and stared into the dark night, but the frigid air and noises broke into the room. I tensed. Then, I noticed something in the middle of the backyard.

Two gleaming eyes viewed me from the darkness. A forest animal? Raccoons and foxes usually never stepped so close to my house—we had no shiny goods or chickens to steal. Wild primroses grew in the meadow—sometimes, they attracted rabbits and does.

The dazzling eyes neared me slowly. Somebody was coming, somebody much shorter than a human but big enough for a creature. I was unable to look away. It indeed had to be an animal. Maybe a wild boar? I was safe behind the window, so I leaned closer to have a better look. And then... I couldn't believe it, but I knew I wasn't wrong.

I dashed outside the house and stood in the rain. I fell on my knees, reaching my hands out desperately. He approached me—he took slow and fearful steps closer, and when he started rushing to me faster, I could see his tail in the dim light. My eyes didn't lie.

I embraced his frame, stroked his fur and even kissed the wet muzzle. It was Dodger. Damp and dirty, but he returned home.

"Dodger," I whispered into his ears. Dodger, my labrador retriever, whined silently and licked my face. "Dodger, where's Agris, little buddy? Is he in the woods?"

"Let's go home, Dodger." He followed me obediently. I comforted him, "I'll reed you."

A moment later, Dodger munched a sausage that I managed to find in my fridge. I stood by my pet, thinking about what to do.

The dog existed. I hadn't imagined Dodger.

Yet, I had to ensure the dog wasn't just my imagination. Calling Paula or my parents at such a late hour would be a mistake. I know what they'll say. They'll accuse me of kidnapping somebody else's pet in my despair. I required only one week to realise that anything was possible in this life. Paula saw Dodger during the dinner that night, but knowing her, she will deny it. All of them said I never owned a dog.

Yet, there was another person who knew about Dodger's existence. My neighbour. She couldn't have missed seeing a dog in my backyard. When I left the house, Dodger happily followed me, but I couldn't see any lights in my neighbour's windows. She had to be home because her Passat was parked by the house. It was late already, but that other time she visited me at night, too.

I stopped by the entrance. An embarrassing memory resurfaced in my mind—the moment I stood here with Inspector Vitols. It was clear Aya considered me insane.

When I knocked, Aya opened the door only ever so slightly.

"Laura?"

"Good evening," I smiled. "My dog has returned. Dodger," I continued smiling and viewing her triumphantly. "The same one that doesn't exist. The same one you've never seen, just like my husband.

"I don't know what you're talking about," Aya replied.

"You told the inspector that you've never seen my husband nor my dog!" I continued examining her closely. "But you knew Dodger. He sometimes runs to you while you tend your garden."

Aya opened the door wider and glanced over my shoulder. She noticed the dog. As soon as Dodger saw the open door that led towards the warmth, he approached Aya and poked her with his snout. He probably expected her to pet him.

Did it only seem that way, or was she about to surrender to my fierce arguments? For a moment, it felt like she could say something important—something that would explain the absurd that had taken over my lift. But she didn't.

"Give me a second, please," she said and disappeared

behind the door. A moment later, Aya returned to hand me a visit card.

"I'm a psychiatrist," Aya explained in a stern voice. "I have a feeling you need my assistance. I can help you to solve everything."

Aya Versite. Psychiatrist, the visit card proclaimed.

"Do you think I'm insane?"

"I don't use such words in my profession," she said nonchalantly.

"I'll consider it," I replied and turned to leave. I had to tame my tears before she'd notice them.

"I work in Tukums clinic every day from nine to one o'clock," Aya continued. "If you're looking for help, feel free to reach out to me out of my working hours."

"I'll consider it!" I hissed, feeling offended. "Dodger, buddy! Let's go home!"

The dog followed me obediently.

"Laura!" the neighbour called my name when I was already a few steps away from her.

I turned around.

"I wanted to tell you about the dog," she said very carefully as if fearing my reaction. "A new family with kids has moved into the twin houses. They came here today, looking for their pet—a sand-coloured labrador retriever. He ran away, and the children are utterly upset."

"The same as my Dodger?" I snickered sarcastically.

"I think you should return their dog. It belongs to that family."

I started laughing. I didn't feel the humidity and cold

weather because I was fuming with anger. They all think I'm ill. Maybe they even convinced me that my husband doesn't exist, but nobody will convince me to abandon my dog. Dodger is mine. My dog, dammit! He came home, responding to his name. He obeyed my commands and behaved the exact way he did a week ago.

"Dodger is mine, and I won't give him to anyone. Good night!" I answered proudly before leaving.

CHAPTER SIXTEEN

It was challenging to wake up the following day, and the air seemed suffocating after the nightmares. I craved a cup of coffee and some fresh air. After opening the bedroom window, I inhaled the fresh breeze of air deeply, wishing I had more strength. After putting on my pale blue jeans and the soft brown sweater, I walked downstairs. The phone notified me that I had multiple missed calls from my parents, but it wasn't the time to return the call. Dodger stood by the door, viewing me with a begging stare.

"Buddy, promise me you won't run away again," I caressed his head and remembered that I should buy some dog food for him. Also, I had to find a job. "Wait for a little while longer."

Outside the garage, there should be another leash hanging on the wall. The dog glanced at me as I pulled on my coat, walked outside the door, and left him on his own. I noticed a police car approach my house. Another car appeared after it.

Maybe they've found Agris?

Both cars stopped by the road. Inspector Vitols got out of the police car, but a woman and a man left the other vehicle. Both seemed like in their forties. The female wore a white, fluffy coat, and she had brown hair with a short bob haircut. As soon as she noticed me, she seemed irritated and angrily said something to the man.

"Good morning, Laura," the inspector greeted me from afar. His voice was cold as if talking to a bank robber. I stepped back towards the door, feeling threatened.

"What do you want from me?" I yelled to express that I didn't expect any guests. "Have you found my husband?"

"So she really is crazy," I heard the man whisper to the woman by his side as they moved towards me.

"Laura, we have a different issue here. I hope we can solve it peacefully," the police officer came closer, but I grasped the door handle to show him that I could disappear any moment.

The inspector halted. He rose his arms, seemingly to calm me. "Laura, please return the dog to these people as they're the rightful owners. We know the retriever is in your house. Their kids are waiting for their pet."

"Dodger is my dog! He's mine! My husband and I took him from a shelter. You have no right to come here and demand me to give him away!"

"Laura, I beg you! Let's solve this peacefully," the policeman suggested. "There's a person who saw you with someone else's dog. This family moved into one of the twin houses only a few days ago, and their dog ran away."

"The dog responds to his name—Dodger—and he

recognises me," I said. "How would you explain that?"

"Listen, you! Give us our dog back," said the man who kept his mouth shut until now. He came closer. "The labrador's name is Bono, and he's our family's dog for the past eight years."

"How old is the dog?" I asked only to earn myself some more time. I needed a moment to distract him.

"Dmmit, woman! Bono is nearly nine years old!" the man yelled.

"Please, return our dog," the woman spoke. "Our children are crying the entire morning. Please, be humane!"

I opened the door and called for Dodger to show them that the dog obeys my commands. Dodger ran outside, seemingly perplexed as he glanced at everyone. Then, he whined and rushed to the strange couple. The woman squatted and hugged the dog, but the man patted his back.

I froze, unable to say a word. The dog recognised the strangers.

"Thank you, Laura!" The inspector came near me and whispered, "I'll ensure this family doesn't press charges for kidnapping their pet. You did everything right this time."

I remained mute. My eyes felt sore as I attempted to tame my tears.

Everyone left, and I watched Dodger follow the family of strangers willingly. When the dog jumped into the back seat, his owner spared me one last glance. It was full of pity and scorn. The police officer was craftier with his examinations— he viewed me from the corner of his eye as if I had grown a pair of wings or horns. That's how strange their attention felt.

Everyone departed, and I took my neighbour's visit card out of the pocket. I called the number on the card while looking at the neighbour's house and windows. Aya was nowhere near them. She picked up the phone after a few rings.

"I'm listening," she acknowledged.

"Aya, this is Laura. Your neighbour," I gasped.

"Laura!" she sounded surprised, "how can I help you?"

"I gave the dog away, Aya," I muttered. "I gave away the dog that never belonged to me.

"It was the right choice, Laura," she replied.

"I was thinking about your proposal. I'd like to receive your help. I need a doctor."

"That's another good choice, Laura," Aya reassured. "Would you like me to come by tonight?"

"That would be lovely."

"I'll see you later then," she ended the conversation.

Before Aya's arrival, I forced myself to be busy. I took a hot shower, prepared a proper meal, treated my dry face with a hydrating cream, cleaned the house. But as soon as I glanced outside the window and noticed my neighbour rushing to my house, I got anxious.

My mysterious neighbour turned out to be a psychiatrist. I'd often wondered what she did for a living and when she wasn't tending her garden or stalking me through her windows. Now I find out she's a doctor for mind and spirit. Agris was a man who existed only in my head. He had a handsome face with precise details—a cleft chin, a birthmark next to his left ear, the way his jaw tightened when he was angry. I recognised the scent of his cologne that he used since

79

the beginning of our relationship. He'd exercise by lifting dumbbells by the window every morning, then go to work. He'd come home, have dinner with me and walk the dog afterwards. We'd make love by the yellow night lamp. Sometimes, he'd be nervous when things went wrong at work, but I never had to suffer from it.

Oh, god, Agris was so real in my head—as real as my hair, ears, hands and feet. I could touch him, after all. Was it even possible to help me? Could a woman who tends her garden wearing tattered jeans help me? Yet I must try. I know the world is against me, and nobody aside from this woman wants to help me. After all, there must be an answer to why Agris is so realistic in my mind. Are those just my fantasies?

I offered her a cup of coffee, but Aya refused. We made ourselves comfortable in the living room, sitting in the armchairs across from each other. Aya's expression was unreadable, but then I realised—she's no longer my neighbour, she's my doctor, and I'm her patient now.

"The past few days haven't been easy for you, have they?" she began. Her eyes seemed to examine me, but there were no pity or compassion in her gaze. I wanted to talk because there was no other way to express my emotions.

"Honestly, my life has come to the situation where Google can't solve my problems," I chuckled, and she smiled back at me. "I can't believe my husband doesn't exist. There must be a logical explanation for everything that's happened.

"Do you believe your husband will return?" she asked.

"Yes," I answered honestly. "But I have no clue how he'll explain everything to me."

"Laura, would you mind if we talk about you instead of your husband today?" Aya suggested unexpectedly. "I'd like to get to know you better."

"What would you like to talk about?" I was surprised.

"About you," she said without any hesitation, "I'd like to talk about you and only you."

"Well, I've discovered that I'm not normal and that I've imagined myself a husband and a dog."

"Has anything happened during your childhood? Anything that you can't forget?" Aya asked suddenly.

I watched the bare ash tree trio behind the window. It was good for them to be together—being alone was hard. Asking about childhood traumas is probably every psychologist's duty.

Suddenly, I heard strange sounds as if somebody had opened a tap to let the water run somewhere. Without mentioning a word to Aya, I stood up and walked out of the room to investigate the kitchen, but it was fine. I peeked inside Agris's office, but nothing there either. I returned to Aya. She pretended not to notice my strange behaviour.

"I gad to check..." I confessed quietly. "I truly trust he will come home, so I respond to every single sound I hear."

Aya nodded.

"I got lost in the woods once," I told her when I took my seat. "I was only seven years old. A military man found me on the third day in the evening."

Aya wrote something down in her notebook, but she didn't say anything. I waited for her to ask me something more about the fragment of my childhood, but instead, she asked,

"Did you blame anyone for what happened?"

"Of course not," I replied, stunned. "It wasn't my parents' fault. It was my own. I got offended by my sister, so I ran into the forest without thinking about the consequences."

"Laura, were you supposed to think about the consequences?" Aya continued immediately. "As a seven-year-old?"

"Are you trying to convince me that I should blame my parents instead?" I smiled.

"No," Aya replied. "But you weren't supposed to take responsibility for what happened."

"But it was my fault!" I objected. "I was seven. I was big enough to realise that running into a forest on my own would be dangerous."

"You were a child," Aya comforted. "People tend to take responsibility for their childhood mistakes, although we shouldn't. Unfortunately, our childhood never really leaves us. What we experience as kids stays with us for the rest of our lives."

"Has anything similar happened to you when you were a child?" I wondered.

I wanted to get to know her closer. Suddenly, I noticed that my neighbour was quite an attractive, well-groomed woman. Her hair was neat, pinned in a high bun with a gorgeous amber hair clip. I liked her ascetic white blouse and classic black trousers. It made me remember a motto I once heard from a stylist who was about to publish a book when I worked at the typography. It said, "Darling, you can never get wrong when wearing a white blouse."

Aya smiled, but it was a sad type of smile.

"No, nothing similar happened," she confessed. "But there was an event that still follows me today.

"I suppose you're not going to tell me about it, are you?" I smiled back. "Psychiatrists don't tell their patients about their private lives."

"Why? Aya raised her eyebrows. "To achieve results, I must be open with my patients. Maybe we could move to the kitchen, and you can make me a cup of coffee? I'll tell you everything afterwards."

"Yes, of course," I said, attempting to his my surprise. We went to the kitchen. I walked behind Aya, thinking about her unusual approach to her work.

I poured some water into the kettle and waited for the water to boil while she made herself comfortable at the table.

"When I was nine, my three-year-old brother unexpectedly choked on a slice of meat by the dinner table," Aya began talking quieter than before. "His eyes widened as his breath got stuck. Panicking, our mother tapped his back because every second was crucial. Fearfully I watched my mother do it, confident that everything would turn out okay. Mom acted as if she'd been trained for such events; she stood in front of me, pressing on my brother's chest and then... Complete silence. Whispering, she asked me to leave the kitchen and not come back. My brother's face was frozen, pale, but his frail hands no longer moved. The last thing I remember is how Mom took him tightly in her arms, stroking the wet hair away from his forehead."

I was unable to say a word.

Aya continued a while later.

"My parents got divorced after what happened. Dad blamed Mom," Aya explained, and a trail of tears trickled down her cheek. She blinked, then continued in a distant voice, "I heard my father criticise my mother, saying that she had made the meat chunks too big, blaming her for not teaching her children to chew the food properly, calling her a bad mother and a stupid woman. He rebuked her for not calling the ambulance in the first place. I don't think we even had a phone back then, so she would have to visit the neighbours to make a call—and they didn't live that close."

"Was your father that pitiless?" I couldn't believe it. "Blaming your mother for the child's death! It was an accident!"

"When people are hurt, they tend to protect themselves that way. By blaming others, although it's pointless," Aya replied and took the cup of coffee. "Mom tortured herself with self-accusations that eventually killed her. She got ill with cancer. I'm confident that the guilt resulted in her illness."

"Are you trying to say I should stop blaming myself for my childhood accident?"

"Exactly," Aya answered. "It's nobody's fault. It's more important that everything ended well in your case."

I tried to grasp Aya's words. That moment, I realised that I had stopped thinking about Agris for a while.

"That's it, for today!" Aya stood up, thanked me for the cup of coffee and strode towards the exit.

I was confused. How? Was it over? Aren't we going to talk about Agris?

"I'll pay you," I said, following Aya.

"Laura!" Aya turned to face me when she was already by the door. "I'm not going to take any payments from you for this chat. But thank you. I could come by tomorrow again."

I nodded, and she disappeared behind the door.

For a moment, I watched her leave—confidently, without looking back.

CHPTER SEVENTEEN

A real autumn storm began in the evening. Bright thunder shot through the clouds, turning the stormy sky into scornful faces. Never in my lifetime had I felt as cold as now, although the house was warm—I turned on the electric hearth. Anxiety that tormented me from within seemed eager to attempt to return life into my lifelessly frozen body. In addition, one persistent question kept throbbing in my head— were the recent events real or just awful nightmares? The noise of the rainfall behind the windows wouldn't let me recollect my thoughts for an answer.

My parents' car appeared by the house before seven o'clock. Avoiding their arrival was no longer possible. My mother would call me ten times a day, and my father insisted on visiting me. Paula made excuses that she was busy at work, but I knew the truth—she didn't care about me nor how I felt. She wasn't bothered if I were ill with schizophrenia or if my nightmares had vanished.

For a while, after getting out of their car, my parents stood in the rain under my mother's umbrella and discussed something. They didn't suspect that I was watching them through the living room window. My father's face looked rough—even cruel—in the dim light from the lanterns. The rain dripped down his back, but despite the cold weather, Dad rigorously kept explaining something to Mom. Theatrically, she motioned with her hands before moving towards the entrance of my house, leaving Dad alone in the rain. I moved away from the window to avoid getting noticed. Then, I went to greet her.

When Mom and Dad entered the house, both acted as if nothing significant had happened—as if I were a normal grown-up daughter that they're simply visiting.

We acted as if I hadn't lost my mind and come up with an imaginary husband.

"It's a proper storm tonight," Dad complained as he walked in and shook off the trails of rain. He held two large bags full of various food items in his hands.

Mom came to embrace me immediately, and I froze in her arms for a moment. My mother smelled differently. Could it be because she hadn't baked any cakes during the day? I always thought she smelled only of vanilla and cinnamon since I was a kid.

"Darling, have you considered moving to Riga yet?" Mom poured her questions down me as soon as she removed her wet coat. "Your father and I will help you. You can live with us at the beginning."

"No, I wish to stay here," I replied sternly without any hesitation. I needed them to see my opinion couldn't be changed or manipulated. "I want to stay in the Woodwalks."

My mother didn't respond. Instead, she followed Dad into the kitchen. They acted as if they were in their own house, but I could understand their behaviour. After all, this once used to be their home.

"I have no food here," I explained immediately.

"You don't have to worry about it," Dad replied proudly. "We've bought enough food to last a week. Look at you! You're only skin and bones now!" He inspected me with a worried gaze.

"I found a good psychiatrist," I announced to change the subject. "She's my neighbour and lives nearby. She moved in recently."

"A neighbour? Are you sure she's a doctor?" Mom inquired sceptically.

"I've reached out for help—isn't that the most important?"

"Yes, of course, it is!" Mom replied promptly.

"Are you planning to return to work?"

"Yes, certainly. I'm planning to send out my CV soon."

"See, Mara? I told you our girl would be fine!" Dad noted enthusiastically, but I couldn't help but notice that his expression was grave rather than happy.

A while later, Mom was rushing through the kitchen, making something by the stove. Dad went for a smoke by the lobby window.

"I'll prepare some quick dinner for you," Mom announced. "Your favourite macaroni and cheese. You used to be crazy about macaroni and cheese when you were little, remember?"

"Mom, did Paula have any objections when you decided to give this house to me?" I asked nervously and avoided my mother's gaze. The question had bothered me for a long while, but I had no clue how to ask it without displaying that I also had black holes in my memories. I couldn't recall why I lived in my parents' home. In my imaginary world, the house was a wedding gift.

Honestly, I was no longer sure what worried me the most because there was another thing I failed to explain—how was it possible that I left my work at the typography? I couldn't understand it. If I had no husband, then there were no plans about conceiving a baby either—then how come I left the job I loved so much? I started considering that the management dismissed me because of my strange behaviour. They probably noticed that I'm not normal. Maybe I told them about my imaginary husband and a dog... and they found out I live on my own. So they decided to get rid of me.

So, I kept telling myself: I lost my mind.

Mom placed down the kitchen knife and glanced at me.

"Your sister has always wanted to live in Riga only, so she didn't mind." I noticed Mom's suspicious gaze. She could feel something was wrong. Maybe everything was becoming much worse.

Dad returned to the kitchen. He pulled the chair closer with a militant movement and sat by the table, staring at me while Mom continued cooking dinner. It felt like a lengthy interrogation would follow to see if I was getting any better.

Instead, he asked, "It's Christmas soon. Are you going to visit us in Riga?"

"Christmas is still far away," I smiled. "But of course, I'll visit you."

"It's always the best time to be together," Mom noted. "Last Christmas, Paula went to the Alps, but you were ill and didn't want us to visit you. This year, Paula promised to participate. I remember how we all had a Christmas eve two years ago. We played Monopoly, talked for hours until the sunrise."

"Excuse me. I'll be right back," I said and rushed to the bathroom, locking the door behind me. Horror took over my bones after hearing Mom's words. I squeezed my mouth shut with both palms to avoid retching. Then, I rinsed my face in cold water and glanced at the mirror. A pale, exhausted expression looked back at me.

Have I lost my mind? I have! I've lost my mind!

I remember that Christmas, but it's different in my memory. We played Monopoly at my parents' apartment in Riga, but Agris and I disappeared until the sunrise. How could have I imagined it? How could I be that ill?

Finally, everything became clear. My parents tried their best not to hurt me, but I had lost the last traces of my sanity.

I'm ill.

I returned to the kitchen and sat down by the table in my usual spot. Mom placed a plate with dinner in front of me. Dad ate silently, yet I could see him examining me from the corner of his eye.

"Darling, what's the matter? Are you unwell?" Mom stood from the table worriedly.

"No, I just got dizzy. Probably it's because I haven't been

eating well lately."

A long pause followed.

They sat on the other side of the table from across from me. I glanced at Mom secretly. A tear trickled down her left cheek, betraying her thoughts. Immediately, another teardrop followed her on the right side. She wiped both trails imperceptibly.

"I remember how you got lost in the woods when you were little," she confessed, but it wasn't her normal voice. It wasn't even a whisper—more like a strangled sound as she tried not to cry. "Our poor baby. You were only seven. On the next morning, there was an unexpected storm. I still can't stand hearing the thunder—it reminds me how my baby was completely on her own in the dark forest, helpless and scared. And if you weren't found on time...."

I placed my palm on Mom's cold hand.

"Of course, you'd find me!" I tried to calm her, although I had no clue what would've happened. I remembered the time in the forest so clearly. Ironically, that one wasn't my fantasy. My childhood trauma was real—well, at least something in my life was authentic.

"Yes," Dad added. "Laura's right. We would've found her because we never stopped looking for our daughter." Suddenly, Dad seemed eager to change the subject as he said, "By the way, do you remember how you feared ghosts when you were a kid? You used to love telling us some horror stories!"

"Is that so?" I chuckled as I started remembering something. I was probably ten back then.

"Yes, yes! You even came up with a ghost family that lived in the same room with you and Paula. Your sister was furious with those stories. She'd come to us during nights because you frightened her."

"Oh, that's right! Paula's horrified face is something I'd never forget," I laughed with Dad, and Mom finally smiled, too.

After the dinner, Mom tried to force me to try another meal that my parents had brought with them. I watched her cut some meatloaf into perfect slices, put them onto wholemeal bread and decorate it with cherry tomato halves.

"One more sandwich, and I'll have fed you," Mom giggled, sliding another slice my way, and I took it obediently.

"Darling, maybe we should stay over?" Dad suddenly offered.

"Dad, it's not necessary," I said. "Really."

Then, my mother spent a moment telling us about a strange order she had received for some hen night. Her clients wanted the cake in a shape of a penis. Mom had been looking for photo examples for the cake when Dad walked into the room, and then... I didn't hear the rest because, honestly, I wasn't paying attention. It was only a muffled sound as if somebody had stuck cotton buds in my ears. My parents laughed. I even giggled a little—just to make them believe I listened to the story. It was all a lie.

Something wasn't right. Something went against everything I used to know and think. Then, I realised I was too tired to express how unwell I felt.

Ten minutes to eleven, my parents left, and I walked them

to the front door. I had to promise them multiple times that I'd go to bed soon and keep my phone near so they can reach out.

I woke up before eight in the morning because I was desperate to pee. Still sleepy, I slid to the bathroom. I squinted like an owl because of the fluorescent lights, and I suddenly registered the contradiction that had visited my mind last night.

If I've imagined my husband and he didn't exist—then why did he feel so real? Why did I suspect my parents—the same as Paula—were hiding something from me?

But I was too sleepy to come up with an answer. Instead, I slid back into my bedroom and lay there for a while. My eyes were half open as I stared at the ceiling, feeling how empty the house was—I could hear every tiniest sound of the wind echoing in my overheated mind. I pondered about all the strange events and how all of them got explained by my illness after losing my job.

There was no logic.

But why would all of them lie?

Then, I noticed the laptop that had been lying on the floor under the dresser. I rushed out of the warm blanket and took the laptop back to bed with me.

I turned it on and got confused. What was my Facebook password? It felt like my brain refused to obey me. I touched the keyboard, and my fingertips remembered the correct letters. As soon as I got inside the platform of virtual friendships, I began examining my profile. I hadn't done it for so long that it seemed like I was looking at a stranger. My status was "married", but there was no information about my husband. So I've done miraculous things when my fantasy overwhelmed me. The album was empty—the only photo was my profile picture taken when I still worked at the typography; I posed, holding a book in my hands. I remembered that moment with the book. It was about travels to India. My friend list consisted of my old colleagues and classmates. I found some strangers, too, but I had no clue who they were or why they were added as my friends. I tried to pay attention to every detail that could help me grasp what was happening in my life, but it was no use. My profile only proved that a boring woman was its owner. It was no surprise she lost her marbles and imagined herself a prettier reality eventually.

And then I noticed it. I had scrolled my Facebook feed for a while when one post hit me like a rock.

Eight months ago, I had created a post about a jeweller named Armands Virbulis, and there was a comment.

"We found wonderful engagement rings at Armands'. We recommend his shop to all new couples."

So I was already in my imaginary world eight months ago!

I was about to close the laptop when I suddenly noticed another thing—a comment. Somebody had added more than just a heart or a smiley face.

The author of the comment was Armand Virbulis—the jeweller.

"Thank you for choosing my rings! It was a pleasure to meet you—Laura and Agris!"

A burst of hysterical laughter escaped my mouth, and I was unable to calm down for several minutes. Clearly, my psyche got tired of crying, so it laughed instead.

***

My fingertips ran over the mobile phone, pressing the numbers I found on Google to reach out to Armands Virbulis.

The jeweller picked up the phone after the third ring. "Armands listening."

I knew this stern, deep voice.

"Armand?" I gasped. "My name is Laura Redlich. I ordered the wedding rings with my husband—Agris Redlich—at your shop."

"Let's assume that's the case," he replied. "But please don't tell me you're another couple that has decided to get divorced after quarantine and wish to return the rings!"

My extended pause probably got translated the wrong way, and Armands started yelling, "I won't do any refunds! You've already bought the rings, and I don't care if you don't love each other anymore!"

I started laughing, although it wasn't the right moment for humour.

"No, we aren't planning to get divorced," I added. "I mean... I wanted to say that—unfortunately—my husband has lost his ring, and we'd like to order an exact copy of what we had for our wedding."

"Then come here and order some. My working hours are on the website," Armands replied, his voice a little softer.

"Could we do it distantly? I'm sure you have the measurements noted down somewhere."

The jeweller sighed.

"Okay, one moment, please. I'll have a look if there's any information about your order on my computer."

I heard his keyboard clicking. The impatience made me

feel like I could lose my mind all over again.

"What was your surname, please?"

"Redlich. Laura and Agris Redlich."

Silence. A tiny squeak on the phone. Another click of the keyboard.

"Found it!" Armands Virbulis announced a few seconds later. "Yes, Laura and Agris Redlich. I have your husband's measurements. You were here on 8 February."

"See!" I replied, feeling pleased. "If I remember correctly, we went there together with my husband, is that right?"

"Dear, I have quite a few visitors every day," the jeweller noted. "But if I have your husband's ring size, I must have measured it here myself. Although..."

"Yes? What did you want to say?" I tried to mask my unease.

"Agris Redlich, did you say?"

"Yes, yes! Agris Redlich! My husband!" I almost screamed.

"I remember your husband. He left a visit card for me in case if I ever required any cargo transfers. He works in logistics, right?"

I inhaled deeply, and my heart trembled.

"Yes, my husband works in logistics."

"Okay, then I remember you both," the jeweller added. "I have the sizes. Should I make a ring for your husband only?"

"Yes, but not now. I must end the call; somebody is buzzing at the door. I'll call you again, Armand," I said.

I sat down on the living room windowsill and stared outside blankly to recollect my anger. The jeweller was my hope. That person had no connections with me. If my parents are lying to me about not knowing Agris, maybe there's a reason why they'd do that. Perhaps something has happened to Agris, and they agreed to this circus to keep me safe?

But most importantly—Agris has been indeed a part of my life. There must be an explanation. Dammit, there's not a single thing in life that couldn't be explained—there are answers to everything, but it's just a matter of digging them up. I jumped off the windowsill and tried to think of things I hadn't examined in this house.

It came to my mind only a few seconds later—we used to hide there when we were kids as we played Hide and Seek. But after I got lost in the woods, Dad locked the place—the attic. The attic of this house.

A moment later, I was at the locked door, trying to break it open. My efforts were useless. The door wouldn't cooperate, although the wood was old and looked thin. I had no key either, and I had no clue where to find it.

But what if somebody hid it on purpose? Somebody who knew what happened. I considered it, and then I came up with a new plan. I went downstairs and outside in the garden. I bolted into the garage and tried to find an axe. It had to be here somewhere. Yes! I found it on the steel shelf.

I rushed back. I decided it was best to avoid Aya's curious eyes, so I disappeared back into the house as quickly as possible. I haltered when I found myself by the attic door again. I had never used an axe in my life, and I didn't even have a clue how to hold it properly.

I smashed the axe into the wood clumsily. The sharp end

got stuck. I had to pull it out forcefully and try again—this time, harder. The hole in the door got larger. I repeated the strikes until the old planks shattered.

I'll find you, Agris. I'll find out the truth, no matter what!

When the hole was larger, my back had gotten wet from the swat. But it took a while longer until the hole was large enough for me to climb inside. The lights in the attic pierced through two dusty windows, but it was enough to avoid looking for a flashlight. I recognised the unique smell of the attic dust as I used to love it when I was a child.

Piles of old furniture and boxes unfolded before my eyesight—probably old enough to be here since the house was built. At first, it seemed like nothing had anything in common with Agris. I felt disappointed, but I decided to open at least some of the boxes. I sat down by the two nearest chests and noticed that they were sealed with tiny locks. I'd have enough strength to break them, but I needed some help from my new friend—the axe.

I have no doubts my parents would immediately call a psychopathic specialist if they saw the scene in the attic. The door was shattered, the locks on the chests got ripped off, the floor was full of Mom's old fur coats and Dad's army jackets and photo albums and magazines from his 'good old times'. Mortification washed over me as I realised how badly I had demolished the place. I even considered having a general cleaning for the entire house tomorrow. I stood up, wiped the dust from my clothing and prepared to leave. But then, I noticed another box on the other side of the broken door.

When I opened the door, everything inside me frosted.

My dear wedding accessories lay before me: the snow-white cushion of our wedding rings, the traditional apron, and my husband's straw hat, but underneath it—there was a wedding photo taken by Polaroid camera. I recognised myself in the picture as I smiled, standing on the terrace of this house. I was wearing a wedding dress with a romantic bell-shaped skirt and a tiara made of flowers, holding a pastel bouquet of peonies in my hands. Oh my god, I must be insane—I had organised an imaginary wedding for myself!

I got nauseous. My stomach twisted like a whirlpool, and I puked, trying to avoid the items in the box. Empty and devastated, I returned to glance inside the box again. This time, I found another curious thing. There was another photo underneath the first one. When I moved the first one away, the second one made me want to scream in horror.

Agris and I—both together.

My husband was stunning on our wedding day. He wore a navy blue suit and a bright smile on his face. He seemed truly happy. He held one hand around my waist, posing enthusiastically—maybe a little theatrically, but his eyes were full of love and joy. It wasn't my fantasy. The photo was real—it existed! I stroked the glossy photograph and remembered everything. It was the morning of our wedding day before we'd go to the registry office.

All of them lied to me!

Agris existed! But what happened? Where is he? Is he dead? Why is my family lying to me?

I was furious about everything they've done to me, about the lies and betrayal and the pain that took over every cell of my body. I no longer cried. I no longer felt sick.

I wanted to take revenge on every single lie. I took both photographs and headed downstairs. In the living room, my gaze landed on the car keys. My parents told me it was my car. God dammit, it was Agrid Redlich's car!

Let's begin with my neighbour. Aya knew the truth about Agris's existence— I had no doubts. That woman earned my trust with wrong moves, pretending to be a psychiatrist and acting her role in this circus to get some money from me for her 'services'.

I took my axe and headed to Aya's house with heavy steps. Her car was by her house. I screamed Aya's name repeatedly. Unless her TV would be louder, there was no way to miss my voice. She appeared by the second-floor window, instantly sensing what to wait for. I could see it in her expression as it flashed behind the window only for a second. Of course, she was scared of me. My clothes were dirty with the dust and spider webs from the attic. I was exhausted, and my nose bled as it usually would from severe stress. But I couldn't care less. I wanted revenge. They deserved it for the lies. Possibly, my husband is dead because of it. I allowed them to convince me that I was insane. I even got drugged!

Liars! Liars! Liars! God damn liars!

My shrills were painful, and I faltered when I lost my voice.

So rose the axe and smashed it against Aya's car.

PART TWO

CHAPTER EIGHTEEN

Almost two years ago

I glanced outside the window of our family's apartment. Twilight painted the air outside, and Christmas decorations sparked new energy at the front of the houses and in the park. Without a rush, Mom set the table and arranged the festive dishes and glasses. An army of Santa's little helpers decorated the Christmas tree. Dad had sat down at the end of the table to read a newspaper while waiting for guests and other family members.

Soon my mother and I brought the snacks from the kitchen. We had everything—the traditional grey peas and sauerkraut, homemade pasties and honey gingerbread. I stepped away to marvel at this scenery. I loved it. Our family valued Christmas, but we'd rarely invite any guests.

"Why's Paula late?" Mom asked as she opened the fridge door to glance at her handmade cake as if anything could happen to it. "We must go to the table soon."

"She called a moment ago. Paula said she's on the way

and the '*the one and only*' is with her," I explained.

Mom took off her apron and laughed. "God, please give us hope that this would truly be the 'one and only', or else it's too much for my nerves."

"Mara, it's not funny," Dad raised his eyes from the newspaper. "Paula must stop introducing us to a new man every six months! I'm surprised she has the nerve to invite him to our Christmas table!" Father murmured angrily.

"Dad, it's okay," I tried to calm my parents. "I spoke to Paula. This one is 'the one' for her."

"They've been together only for a couple of months! What true love is that supposed to be?" he noted sarcastically. "That's not love, Laura."

"Dad, they've known each other for a long while before Paula moved in with him. I honestly believe Paula loves him. It's serious this time."

"I hope that man has a decent job, at least," Dad muttered with no satisfaction and put his glasses back on.

"I doubt my sister would move in with an unemployed man. I doubt it," I joked, enjoying my surprisingly good mood. Honestly, I knew nothing much about Paula's new relationship. We rarely spoke about it. Yet the way she talked about that man convinced me that she had genuine feelings for him. She treasured this relationship. Paula seemed in love.

As for me, I'm a maiden—thirty years old, I've never been married, I haven't even been in a long-term relationship with any man, and I've no children. My sister has no children either. There's no record of her marriage in any of the registry offices, all her cohabiting experiences lasted no longer than a few months, but nobody ever thought of calling Paula a maiden, even though she's older than me.

The difference is probably in the attitude—the way we perceive the meaning of a maiden. Even though there was no new '*the one and only*' in her life now—everything would continue the same way as it always was. Nobody will call my sister a maiden, even when she turns forty or fifty. I, however, felt like one when I turned eighteen. I'm waiting for my 'one and only' too. I know my parents are also waiting for him—at least Mom has mentioned a few hints.

No, of course, I don't feel guilty for having no family and children in my thirties. I don't owe anyone any explanations, but imagine the ridiculous feeling when somebody asks you what your husband or boyfriend does. After explaining the situation, you must be ready to bear the looks like you were some abandoned dog. If you look at life through pink glasses, I've nothing to complain about. I have a fantastic job, amazing parents, and I enjoy living with them. My face is appealing, and I'm lean and healthy. Sometimes men follow me on the streets just to introduce themselves.

Once a month, I go out for some cocktails with two our three of my friends to chat and dance. However... I really, really want to have kids and get married—I just haven't met the right man yet. Nobody has fallen in love with me.

Dear Santa Claus, I know you don't exist, but please, all I want for Christmas is to meet someone special. I'll be grateful even if he won't be every woman's dream. I'll be thankful even if he turns out to be the complete opposite of a dream man. Dear Santa, be loyal—you know I deserve it.

A doorbell rang, and the door got unlocked from outside. Paula's silent chuckling trickled into the room, followed by a man's voice. My parents went to greet them.

"Laura, keep an eye on the oven, will you?" Mom asked

before she went to the lobby with Dad. "The salmon should be ready any moment."

"Okay," I said and stood by the family dinner like a trustworthy guard.

A burst of Dad's laughter came from the lobby, and it was clear that Paula's new boyfriend successfully impressed our parents. They're bad liars. Dad only laughs when the joke is hilarious. He doesn't act in front of any strangers, not even to support a family member. Mom, on the other hand, likes all Paula's boyfriends because Mom loves all people on the planet.

Suddenly, I felt stupid and like I didn't belong here. I was thirty years old, and I hadn't brought a man home to meet my parents—not even once. Mom would try to comfort me, saying there was no rush because she met my father in her more mature years, so she wasn't worried.

Well, I was. It bothered me because I wouldn't be able to conceive a child if my future husband failed to appear in my life any time soon.

I waited for the oven timer to beep, looking outside the window and viewing the falling snowflakes. The guests took ages to remove their coats, and it took an even longer time to find suitable slippers for them. They were busy chatting with my parents, and nobody hurried to meet another family member, although they had to know I was here.

Paula didn't even glance inside the kitchen. Everyone went straight to the living room. I could hear Dad talking about the wine bottles, discussing which one was better—the white wine or the red one. Mom asked everyone to wait for a little because the dinner would be ready soon.

Weren't they going to invite me to join?

A moment later, Mom appeared by the door.

"Laura, turn the oven off. I'm sure the salmon is ready by now. Come, join us in the living room," she encouraged. Then, she whispered, "You must meet Paula's new boyfriend. I like him!"

The timer began beeping, and I had no other choice but to do as Mom said. The living room looked incredibly cosy. Paula had managed to doll up today—she looked gorgeous. To compare with her, I was always just a Cinderella—always busy cleaning and helping Mom in the kitchen, making sure the holiday tables would be set appropriately. I had no time to visit any hairdressers or do my nails.

Paula and her boyfriend sat on the sofa.

I'm unsure why, but I'd imagined that the man would be in his forties—a suitable age for my sister. However, he seemed younger than Paula, and he had a lean, sturdy body. Then, I glanced at him properly.

It'll probably sound banal, but... If I were an author of romance novels, I'd get judged for this cliche story because I froze when our eyes met. This man's gaze gleamed with confidence that bordered with justified arrogance. Yet his eyes remained kind, and he smiled.

"Sister, let me introduce you to my new boyfriend," Paula stood up and grinned widely.

Her man stood up too to approach me.

"Nice to meet you, Laura," he said, reaching out his palm for a handshake. "My name is Agris."

CHAPTER NINETEEN

I sat facing the window. We lived in a house with a magnificent view of the park, so we always kept the curtains open. Since nobody nosy can glance into the second-floor window, we had nothing to worry about. I viewed the grey sky, watching the giant snowflakes slide down festively. It felt like the snow parade was there in my honour because I sat facing both—the window and Agris. Paula was comfortable by his left side, but Mom and Dad were each on the other end. What a wonderful evening.

"Agris, what is your company doing?" Dad inquired, rearranging the food on his plate.

"Logistics services," Agris responded confidently. "We transport cargos all over the world—obtaining, producing, and distributing various materials and products.

"Wow!" Dad gasped. "That's a great business. It must be tough.

"I agree. This type of job carries a lot of tension," Agris noted, and I noticed how Paula smiled after each of his phrases.

"Do you ship food items, too?" Mom asked although she had no clue what logistic processes were.

"Those can be various goods, weighting up to twenty-four tons," Agris told her. "Most cooperation is with legal entities. If we are hired by private individuals, then we are usually dealing with valuable heavy goods, such as exclusive furniture, the transport of sports equipment or even animals."

"Are you from Riga?" Mom continued the interrogation.

"No, I'm from Gulbene," Agris replied. "I went to Riga after high school. The job choices in Gulbene weren't the greatest. Later, I enrolled in the Technical University and studied business logistics."

"What a wise choice," Dad agreed.

Paula looked tired of evaluating the benefits of the logistics profession. I couldn't help but notice that she rejoiced at the exhaustion of the subject. My sister drank several glasses of red wine—one after the other—but nobody seemed to notice the excessiveness apart from me. Unobtrusively, Paula fiddled with the objects on the table, seemingly rearranging them to refill her glass of wine from time to time.

I sat in silence, listening to the conversations and leisurely tasting every snack in a row. Occasionally, I quietly praised my mother for the delicious food. No one paid attention to me, but I was used to it in this family. It didn't hurt me.

Unexpectedly, I was approached by Agris.

"What do you do for a living, Laura?" Paula's boyfriend asked, glancing at me curiously. Suddenly, Paula lifted her eyes from her mobile phone, although she seemed fully submerged in it just a second ago.

"Me?" I faltered for a moment. "I work in a printing house. I help to turn manuscripts into books."

"That's a fantastic job," Agris added. "I dreamed of being a writer when I was younger."

"Seriously? Does anyone even read books these days?" Paula started laughing.

"Of course, they do!" I defended Agris and myself.

"Okay, okay," Paula chuckled. "Don't try to convince me. I'll never read any Latvian novels anyway—only Agris's. I'll be proud of him if he decides to write a book during his free time," she said.

Agris and I glanced at each other. He seemed to begin noticing that Paula was getting tipsy from the amount of alcohol she consumed.

"Agris, would you like another slice of cake? Don't be shy," Mom encouraged, but Agris refused politely.

"The cake is excellent," he responded, "but I'm really full."

"Yes, Agris is careful with maintaining his weight," Paula bragged. "He counts his calories like we—women—do," she added, wriggling in the chair with her wine glass.

"Paula, I don't count my calories," Agris said calmly, but a dissatisfied frown line appeared on his forehead. I kept viewing him, so I noticed every slightest change in his expression.

"Let's raise our glasses and appreciate being together this Christmas!" I suggested to change the subject. "I hope we'll have many more such beautiful holidays!"

All of us stood up as we raised our glasses. Paula's unsteady posture made everyone realise she was drunk already.

Our father pinched his lips shut, our mother lightly shook her head, but Agris was undeniably embarrassed. Everyone pretended that nothing had happened. As usual at any party, they overcome the awkwardness by getting some more food. Paula began complaining that she got tired from work, making excuses that it was the reason why her eyelids felt so heavy. She stood up, vulgarly smiled at Agris, announced that she'd be waiting for him and staggered towards the direction of the bedroom.

The four of us remained in the living room. We talked about all sorts of silly things and joked a lot. My father remembered the Soviet Union era anecdotes that required some reasoning to understand their meaning, but they still made us chuckle. Dad suggested we should play Monopoly, and that entertainment preoccupied us for a couple of hours. With the uplifted mood, we waited for midnight to open the presents. Paula had prepared an old-fashioned blanket for me, and it didn't surprise me at all.

Then, everyone got a little sleepy, so we decided to tidy up the table. Agris announced that he would help and skillfully began to collect the dishes. My father praised him for his logical approach, and it made everyone smile. My parents went to bed, but Agris and I stayed up to take care of a few more bits. I should've probably felt uncomfortable staying alone with my sister's boyfriend while Paula was sleeping in the room nearby, but I didn't care. I wasn't sleepy at all. Agris asked me about working in the printing house, we talked about Latvian writers and went outside on the balcony. I almost slipped on the snow, but Agris managed to grasp my arm. We were so close that I could smell him. Needless to say, I loved his scent. I stepped away politely, but it wasn't what I really wanted at that moment.

"Maybe we should get some more wine? We're not even tipsy yet," Agris suggested. If I knew how to, I'd smile, but I felt suddenly drunker than Paula. Just not from the alcohol.

"Or we could go for a walk instead. Look!" I pointed at the beautiful Christmas lights on the trees down the road. "There's a bench in the backyard. We could sit there with some mulled wine. What do you think?"

"Sounds better than I imagined," Agris replied with a smile on his lips.

The backyard was empty. We swept the snow away from the bench and took some mulled wine in a vacuum flask. Now, it was I who got drunk. I couldn't remember what we talked about, but we chatted all night long. All night. Until the sunrise.

CHAPTER TWENTY

I woke up to the noises around the house. The recent events slowly came back to me only a while later, and I remembered finding evidence of my husband's existence. I also recalled how I smashed my neighbour's—Aya's—car, and how I desperately yelled, calling everyone liars. Then, I called my parents and Paula to let everyone know that I'll never want to talk to them in my lifetime again. Then... *What was next?*

I don't remember.

I examined the photos on the shelf. There was my childhood photo and... Yes, among many other images, there was my wedding photo. How could I forget about it? It was a real photograph. A confirmation. A fact. My muscles tensed, and goosebumps run down my arms.

I know everything that happens in this world has an explanation. Now, I'm considering that maybe Agris got disappointed in me. He was probably going to break up with me and came up with this pathetic show to get rid of me.

Perhaps I deserved it, and maybe I was an awful girlfriend. I'm the evil stepmother's real daughter. I'm an ice queen, not some cute Snow White or some humble Cinderella. I'm an antagonist, not a protagonist. I deprived my sister of love. I stole her man with whom she genuinely fell in love.

I sat on the edge of the bed, unable to get up. My memories broke into my mind, forcing me to remember what I'd done and tried so hard to forget.

"I'm ashamed that you're my daughter," said my mother when the truth came to light. "I didn't raise you to become such a person. Everything will come back to you, Laura! I wish you well, but I'm warning you."

Back then—almost two years ago—my mother's words wounded me. Never before had she spoken to me this way, with such disapproval. Her voice was full of disgust and disappointment.

"Mom, we love each other, and we don't want to resist it!" I shouted at my mother like a fool. I really was like that. I was intoxicated with love towards Agris, and I knew he felt the same way about me. On Christmas Eve, we already realised that Paula was in this world just because she was fated to bring us together. Agris was my destiny.

We met each other the next day while Paula slept through her hangover until lunchtime. Agris had asked for my number, and he sent a text message in the morning, "Good morning! Are you awake already? We could hang out in a cafe. Let me know if you're free, and I'll pick you up."

We sat in a cafe until late evening that day. We got drunk because each other's company made us tipsy. Agris replied only to Paula's first message and showed it to me, saying, "Just so that you know... I want to be honest."

The text message said, "I'm sorry, Paula. I'm sure you'll meet somebody better than me. Sorry."

He didn't read her replies and switched off his ringtone to ensure no sudden sounds of Paula's persistent ringing distracted us. I liked that. This man belonged to me.

"We can stay here overnight. Or should we call a cab? I don't want to drive drunk. What do you think?" he asked.

"Let's stay here," I decided and messaged my mother to say I was staying over at a friend's house.

Since that day, we continued staying together every night. I had Pure's home key on my keyring—Dad and Mom occasionally joked that they would give the countryside house to the first grandchild's parents. At such moments, Mom would smile and add that she was already waiting for too long. Since my parents retired, but Paula and I worked full-time jobs, we used the countryside home only for our holidays. Now the house was empty. Paula's belongings were left in Agris's flat. While they were still there, it felt wrong to move in there. Instead, both of us could live in the countryside and go to work in Riga together.

We lit the fireplace in the Woodwalks and increased the temperature of the central heating. Soon, the house warmed up. We didn't require much. We only needed a bit of food we had taken with us, the sofa in the living room and a few candles and some mulled wine. We had each other for everything else.

It was I who told Paula the truth. It was the last evening

of the Christmas holidays, and we had to go to work the next day. Agris brought me home, we sat in the car by the house, and he asked if he should walk me to the door. I refused—I wanted to tell my family about our relationship on my own. He stayed there in the car to wait for me.

I went up the stairs to our family's flat. Mom rushed out of the kitchen as soon as she heard me turn the key. Her expression was not only full of worries but disappointment. Dad's eyebrows looked genuinely furious.

That moment, Paula appeared with tousled hair by her bedroom door. She smiled disdainfully, holding a glass of wine.

Mom turned to face her. As soon as she noticed the glass of wine in her oldest daughter's grip, she no longer paid attention to me.

"Drinking again?!" she hissed.

The thin glass shattered in Paula's hands. Sliding down on the floor, she continued smiling.

Yes, I must admit that I still feel ashamed to tell myself the truth. I'd love to change something in the past events to ease my guilt because now I understand how selfishly monstrous I was.

Back then, Paula came to consciousness thanks to the smelling salts that Dad put under her nose. Frightened, my sister slapped our father's hand, pushed our mother away from herself and stood up. She faced me with a scornful grimace and tried to spit on me. I avoided it. Her saliva landed on Dad's shirt instead. Paula's anger saved me from the fury of our parents.

"Paula will find herself a new lover, but I'll make this man happy!"

After yelling those words, I rushed to my bedroom to collect my things. I only took what's necessary. Nobody disturbed me. When I left the room, I met my father's gloomy glare. He sat on the small bench in the hallway, looking fatigued and old.

"Dad, I'm sorry," I whispered before kneeling by his side and hugging his broad shoulders. "Should I do to Mom?" I asked fearfully.

"Don't disturb them. I'm sure everything will settle. Go where you wanted to go," Dad encouraged.

Nobody called me—not Dad, not Mom. Not even my sister. Perhaps she bombarded Agris's phone, but he had blocked her number.

"Everything will be okay. Eventually," Agris comforted me and stroked my hair.

My parents called me to announce that Paula was in the hospital because of heavy consumption of alcohol. I told Agris about it and went to see my sister. I noticed the trio approach me by the hospital gate. Paula strolled slowly, taking frail and small steps forwards. It was snowing, and the road was slippery. Mom walked by Paula's side. Dad followed them, and I approached them nervously.

"I wish you died in that forest back then!" Paula shouted as soon as she noticed me. "I don't wish to see you ever again—nor that shit—Agris! You can have him! I curse you both, damned freaks!"

"Paula, calm down. Let's go home," Mom said and took

Paula by her elbow. My sister embraced her tightly.

I had no clue what else to do but to join the trio. In complete silence, we headed to the car park, passing by the snowy puddles.

When we reached Dad's car, I lost my composure. "Paula, I'm sorry! You're so beautiful. You must get yourself together and find a new lover! Agris isn't your man."

Tears began flooding my sister's cheeks, but she remained silent. Dad opened the door for Paula, and she rushed to get inside the car without replying to me. Mom's bitter glare hurt me the most when she glanced at me as they drove away.

I called Agris to let him know I was free.

"Agris, my parents and my sister hate me," I said as I sat down in his car when he arrived to pick me up.

"It's more important that you have them. You have somebody to love, so their hate will diminish soon. Paula will get over it. And don't worry about your parents. They have two kids, and it's normal for parents to express more love to the child who's in bigger trouble.

Back then, I felt like they would never forgive me, but I was wrong.

Something unexpected happened—two months later, Paula called me and offered to meet. When I received her call before lunchtime, I was truly astonished. Parents never called me anymore, and they wouldn't even visit me. So receiving Paula's invitation to meet up for a cup of coffee shocked me.

"I'll never forgive you what you've done to me. But you're my sister, and I don't want to lose you. Besides, our parents seem devastated more than I am. I think we should put an end to it," Paula explained sternly, and her voice was calm as she carefully bit into a slice of cake.

I remained speechless for a moment. It didn't sound like Paula at all. When we were kids, Paula couldn't forgive Dad and me that he gave me the black handbag for my birthday for quite a few years. My sister would never forget if anyone offended her. Perhaps I had to consider it earlier.

However, she convinced me. Paula seemed to have recovered from the pain of my betrayal. She talked to me as if nothing extraordinary had happened. As if I had just taken her lipstick without permission.

"So you live in the countryside house with Agris?" She asked me as if we were best friends. We sat in a cafe near her workplace and stirred the cream in our coffees for a long time.

"Yes," I replied and went quiet.

I still had no clue what to tell her. Sitting across from her, I felt pathetic and miserable. Paula looked gorgeous as always—most likely, she looked much better than I did. Who was I trying to fool? She was always much more stunning than me! Her dark curls billowed down her back, her skin glowed and her perfectly drawn eyebrows seemed like a masterpiece. A couple of lost pounds came handy to her thin waist, and now her breasts were highlighted by the stylishly knitted sweater I had wanted to find for myself for a long while. Externally, I looked more like the one who got abandoned and betrayed.

"Mom and Dad are missing you. It would be best if you come to see them. They love you, Laura," Paula explained calmly and added, "Unfortunately."

"Paula, I know what I've done is unforgivable," I tried to speak, but she interrupted me.

Paula leaned in, grasped my palm and confessed quietly, "Laura. I've finally met the one and only." She grinned playfully. "As it turns out, it had to happen this way with you and Agris to let me meet him. He's truly special!"

"You're in love again?" I asked disbelievingly, yet with a pinch of hope.

"Yes, and that's the reason I'm over Agris," she noted. "I feel nothing for him, Laura. So be happy."

When I arrived at our parents' apartment, Dad embraced me before I even managed to step into the flat. Mom tried to stay away for a moment, but it didn't last long, and she calmed down quickly.

For several months, the idea that Agris would also visit my parents with me seemed quite absurd because Paula still stayed over there. She hesitated to move in with the new "one and only". Asking my parents about my sister's plans seemed impossible—it would be unacceptable because of my recent shenanigans. Questioning Paul about her life seemed equally inappropriate. That's why we postponed everything with Agris until later in the spring when the snow would melt, and the townspeople went on their holidays to the countryside.

And then somehow…

But Paula had different plans. She passionately tried to mend the relationships in our family.

CHAPTER TWENTY-ONE

Three weeks later, Agris and I went to visit my parents. Everything turned out well, although I had a feeling that my parents didn't love Agris. I was happy, and we enjoyed the spring in Pure. It may have been a bit civic, but I had been waiting for it for so long! The guilt of betraying Paula retreated quickly. Everything seemed like a fairy tale with a good ending—they lived happily ever after.

The following Christmas, Agris proposed to me. I agreed without thinking, and that was the beginning. Or maybe the end...

What happened next?

I tried to dismiss the obsessive memories and decided to call Paula. If Agris returns home, we'll all be fine again. Paua's phone was on this time. She picked it up after a few rings, but it seemed like an eternity to me.

"Laura?" She sounded surprised. "Are you feeling better? Maybe I should come to see you? Sorry, the last days at work have been hectic—politely speaking."

"Don't say anything. Paula, please. Just answer me one question honestly, and I will leave you alone."

"Of course, love," Paula replied urgently.

Oh, god, what a charade, I thought to myself. My sister never calls me love.

"Shut up!" I tried to control myself. "Paula, I stole Agris from you. He was your boyfriend, and I destroyed your relationship. You remember it, dammit! Confess!" I screamed into the mobile phone. My free hand curled into a tight fist. "Perhaps it's the most painful thing that's happened in your life. You can't pretend it hasn't happened!"

"Sister..." she said after a while of silence. "Laura, it's becoming dangerous. I'm sorry, but I think our parents are wrong by not seeking professional help for you. Laura, you need a doctor!"

"Give me George's phone number," I requested calmly.

"What?!"

"You heard me. You weren't alone the night when Agris disappeared. George was with you. Dammit, you change boyfriends so often that I don't even know his surname! But he was a witness that Agris was with me."

"Laura, I won't let you contact George. You will embarrass our family even more. The whole Pure is calling you *the crazy maiden living by the highway*"! It is unbearable! Our mother is in bad health, our father is no better. *The crazy maiden by the highway*. Who would dare to call a young and married woman like that?

That hurt me.

"Laura, do you hear me?" Paula continued. "You require

serious help. Please, Laura!"

I hung up the phone and switched it off.

The crazy maiden by the highway...

It hurt me mercilessly.

When I opened my eyes again, it seemed that I had slept all day, but it turned out that it was only eleven in the morning. The landscape outside the window was gloomy and miserable.

How many days ago did Agris disappear? What is the date today? My head seemed dizzy. I touched my forehead to see if it was swollen. No, I could feel the bone through my skin, and my forehead was cool but sweaty. I looked out the window and noticed that there was no Passat in the neighbour's yard. Oh yes, I smashed it. It had to be taken to services, and Aya is currently at work. Maybe I should just go somewhere? Although... When was the last time I was in Riga? I could go to Agris's work. Maybe there's something to find out.

I started thinking about my husband's work. In fact, I don't know much about it because Agris used to mention some things in our conversations, but he never went into details. I've never been to his office either. I wasn't comfortable going there. We lived in the countryside, and I completely immersed myself in enjoying the status of a pampered woman.

I've never visited my husband's office and never attended their events because of Paula. During the few months of living together, Paula often went to Agris's office, visited our parents and me, and she didn't stop talking about the friends she found among her boyfriend's colleagues. My sister also attended a couple of corporate evenings, after which she would praise herself for her talents with everything she touched. Of course, I didn't wish to go to a place where everyone's aware of the evil sister who stole the love of Paula's life.

I told myself that every day must be challenged with a task. Today—I must go to Agris's office, despite the fact that they behaved strangely during our conversation on the phone, claiming that Agris doesn't work for them. I must get up, shower, have some coffee, pick up the car keys and drive.

Looking outside, I decided that I should wear an autumn coat and find a scarf. I shivered in the yard. It's only mid-October, but the air already smells of snow. The cold reminded me to call a central heating engineer. The system must be checked. Agris used to take care of it, but I can't even light a fireplace without him. I do better at lighting candles.

I started the car's engine and drove off. Autumn landscapes are sad. Loneliness scares me, I don't want to have dinner alone, and I don't want to go to bed alone without talking to a close person. I wouldn't want to die single and as a maiden who nobody needed. I should meet up with some feminist who would cheer me up by saying that I'll be able to deal with everything on my own and that I didn't need a man at all.

Maybe I should visit my mother and father as well? Make a surprise? I decided to do it later.

The rift that arose between my mother and me after what had happened to Paula never really healed. Our mother loved both of us, but this is how it is arranged: the mother's heart always cradles the one who suffers the most. And in that relationship triangle—Paula, Agris, Laura—the loser was Paula.

On one of the few occasions when I visited my mother, she started a long mature conversation.

"Laura, listen to me! You will never build your happiness at the expense of somebody else's disaster," she blamed me when we were alone in the kitchen.

I didn't know what to reply. Paula had her "the one and only" for a while now, which, of course, she adored. Agris and I lived in the Woodwalks, and I didn't hide from my mother that we love each other. We lived in harmony. It seemed to me that all was going well. It was time for a new beginning, which my family supported.

"Paula's not interested in Agris anymore, Mom," I replied. "Why are you talking about it again?" I objected to my mother as calmly as possible.

She sat down at the kitchen table, put a towel on the next chair next to her and looked at me as if she had been waiting for this conversation for a very long time.

"In a good family, you will never give up on each other. I believed that I'd raised you well enough to instil at least those basic values in you, Laura," my mother said. "We don't know what is going on in Paul's head. Maybe she still loves Agris, and her peace is just a self-defence mechanism against deeper suffering. She loved that man, Laura. Very much."

I remember taking a deep breath and trying to come up with the right words so that there would be no argument between my mother and me. What was she thinking about when lecturing me about it? Agris and I have shown that our happiness is real, and we look at each other as life partners, not some temporary passion. Paula's men are just entertainment. I know that I haven't done the right thing, but it's been a long time, all of Paula's hysteria has subsided.

"You know that Agris and I will love each other and will get married soon," I reminded my mother. "What do you think—should we order any special decorations for the backyard of the country house for the wedding day?" I tried to change the topic of conversation.

Mom pursed her lips and turned to look outside the window.

"Do as you see fit. You are my daughter, and I will always support you. It's also my fault that you made a serious mistake by starting a relationship with Agris."

I glanced at my mom's profile. She had aged quite a bit during the year, and no cosmetics could smooth out the wrinkles as they became deeper and deeper. Then, she looked at me. Mom's eyes radiated stubborn sadness.

I tried to call my mother because suddenly I yearned to be by her side, but she didn't answer. I know that on weekdays she spends a lot of time at the bakery where she once worked. She's sometimes called for help if there are too many orders. If Mom bakes cakes, then she doesn't touch the phone for several hours.

Oh, how good it would be to fall into Mom's arms—the wave of warmth, security and strength.

Is everything I remember about Agris and Paula the invention of my imagination? My parents, Paula and strangers claim that nothing like this has ever happened: Paula doesn't know any Agris, and she certainly hasn't had a relationship with a man who then became her sister's husband. Everything that I now remember is the fruit of my imagination. Large, heavy fruit.

They're lying. Both—the strangers and my family are lying. They won't convince me that I'm sick. I'll no longer allow anyone to tell me that Agris doesn't exist. I couldn't have imagined him.

The photo of Agris and me on the wedding day was on the passenger's seat in my car. I glance at it from time to time to remind me of today's task. I drove onto the highway and turned in the direction of Riga. I drove past the twin houses. There were no other cars on the road, and I returned to the world of my thoughts. Only at the last moment did I notice some movement to the right side. Oh god, I had steered the car too far to the side of the road, almost knocking down pedestrians—a man and a woman who were walking in the same direction with a sand-coloured labrador.

I stopped so suddenly that the car almost collapsed. Anger rushed to my veins. The pedestrians had to know that the car was approaching from behind. They had to step aside.

It was only now that I noticed that two young children were standing in front of both adults, a boy and a girl, who were holding each other's hands in fright and were now looking at me, their tiny mouths gaping.

I opened the window and addressed the adults. "You should set an example for your children and take a step aside when the car approaches," I said out loud. The woman and the man looked up. The man was holding a dog on a leash, which, when he saw me, began to whine. The man soothed the dog and then turned to me.

"You need to drive on the road, not the ditch. Who issued your driving licence? Don't you dare to approach our dog or us anymore," the man barked in an angry voice as he stepped closer to the car.

I was stunned.

"I don't remember ever seeing you at all," I replied. "I meet you for the first time."

"Rita, go to the house," the man said to the woman, and she grabbed the children and walked away towards one of the twin houses.

The man leaned quickly against my car window again and said to me in a threatening voice, "I won't allow you to endanger my family. You were lucky that this cop persuaded me to withdraw the charges against you."

What the hell is he talking about? Who is he? What charges is he talking about? I see this person for the first time in my life.

"You're confusing me with someone else," I was about to resume driving, confident he would step aside. As the car began to move, the man started walking faster, holding on to the open window of my car.

"We've already been warned that one of the locals here is completely insane, but we didn't think that you were so sick and would try to steal our dog."

"You've lost your mind!" I tried to close the window, but the man's hand had gripped the glass.

It was only when the glass began to press on the man's hand that the stranger snatched his hand back.

I tried to take a deep breath and exhale and not think about the psychopath.

Did that person know me? That couldn't be true. I would like to know who spread such unpleasant rumours. I don't remember ever seeing the strange family nor their dog. Apparently, they've bought one of the twin houses and now live there.

CHAPTER TWENTY-TWO

During the trip, my mood improved a bit. I think. It isn't good to sit at home all day. I'll get even more tired of sitting like that, and only disastrous thoughts will stir my head.

The landscapes behind the window were still, sorrowfully grey. The whole world was so full of indifference that it would last forever. I didn't see any other cars, and it felt like no one in the world existed except me.

Behind the roundabout near Tukums, the traffic became more lively. I drove carefully because I suddenly felt overwhelmed by insecurity. When I got to Riga, I clung to the stirring wheel. Strange anxiety tore my senses.

I stopped the car by the office building that the navigation indicated as my destination. The building stood out against the grey background of the area. As soon as I got out, a sharp wind began to rip the corners of my thin autumn coat. It started to drizzle again, and I tightened the belt around my waist. At the entrance door of the three-storey building, I saw a row of signs with company names.

VINTORS LTD, the international cargo transportation,

announced one of the plates. The exterior door of the building turned out to be closed, but next to it, there was an intercom with a slightly slanted "Call Us" sign. I pressed the button and waited frozen. The door lock clicked, and I got inside, away from the unpleasant moment.

There was no one in the spacious ground floor lobby. The office was on the left, but at least it was marked by an inscription on the modest oak door with a luxurious handle. Behind the door, there was a narrow, long room with white walls and several tables, where men and women sat with microphones and headphones. Only after a moment did they notice the entrant. A tall young woman emerged from the adjoining room in a shapeless but modern dress that almost reached the ground.

"Good afternoon. How can we help?" she asked, squinting with her short-sighted eyes.

I glanced at the room. Apart from the tall woman, four employees sat here. I saw these people for the first time. They were Agris's subordinates. Do any of them know me?

"Good afternoon. My name is Laura Redlich," I spoke convincingly, and it didn't go unnoticed that everyone's eyes turned to me with great curiosity.

The freckled redhead behind the folder-laden office desk looked scared. I noticed her teenage hands clenching the armrests of her chair.

Does she know me?

The woman didn't say a word, waiting for an explanation of why I was there.

"I'm looking for Agris. Agris Redlich," I continued slowly, watching her and the others react.

"The person you're looking for doesn't work for us," the

woman replied convincingly after a moment. "Unfortunately, we won't be able to help."

I knew they would say that!

Nothing surprised me anymore. I had been waiting for such a reaction because even my parents deny that they know Agris. But I had already managed to notice that the woman was nervous. She was a bad actress and a useless liar. Somebody else saw it too. A man, about forty years old. He got up from his seat by the window and approached me in quick steps. I tried to find something familiar in his face, but I failed. Agris had not introduced me to any of his colleagues.

"Good afternoon. My name is Eric," the man stretched his warm palm to greet me. "Unfortunately, no one named Agris works in this company. Perhaps you've mixed up the business premises?"

"I haven't," I replied convincingly. "I came to Vintors Ltd, didn't I?"

"That's correct," the male replied awkwardly.

"Then you must know Agris Redlich, the director of this company," I continued.

"Our director is currently out of office. His name is Karlis Bankovskis," the man replied. "Madam, perhaps you have confused the office premises? We have a wholesale company next door."

"Is that so?" I said without looking away from him. The other employees behind him listened to our conversation and pretended to be working. "In that case, I'd like to become your customer."

"Sorry?" The man frowned in confusion. It seemed that the red-haired woman behind me chuckled after hearing me.

"I need a transportation service, and I want to become

your customer," I repeated. "It's possible, isn't it?"

"Umm, yes, of course," the man answered awkwardly and turned to the other employees. "Sandra, do you have time to take care of the customer?" He held out his hand towards one of the women sitting further away from the others. She didn't pay attention to our conversation, and she was the only one who hadn't raise her head when I came in.

Sandra nodded, got up and came closer.

"Good afternoon! My name is Sandra. Please come with me to the room where we can talk," she pointed at the door on the right.

I felt my heart beating faster. It seemed to me that I'd seen this woman in an ascetic costume somewhere before. She was like one of Paula's schoolmates. We entered a separate room, and Sandra closed the door behind her. There was a lonely table with a computer and two chairs.

"Please, sit down," the woman pointed at the chair. "What exactly are your requirements?" she asked professionally.

The lies about my need to carry cargo were the only way to stay in this office longer. I was already used to the fact that everyone except the jeweller considered me mad. I had to change my tactics. If I continue to say that I'm looking for a non-existent man, I will sooner or later get imprisoned in a psychiatric clinic.

I had to think two steps ahead and be smarter this time.

I tried to speak convincingly, "My husband and I decided to move to Riga, and we need help moving some goods. We live nearly ten miles behind Tukums.

"Yes, of course. We can do that for you," she said in a resigned voice. I realised that I couldn't hope to get on their VIP client list with this little need.

"Great! Then I'll definitely use your services," I kept lying. "We will move next week. Is there anything I need to do before that?"

"What will be the approximate size of the load? We must understand what transport to send you."

"We have furniture and household appliances. One van should be sufficient."

For a moment, I listened carelessly to Sandra's story about the costs of transportation services, nodded and tried to smile. At the end of the conversation, it seemed to me that we had both understood that I required no cargo transfer services. I'm a terrible liar. But Sandra was an expert—she behaved professionally and tried not to spoil the image of her company.

Agris would have hired employees like Sandra.

I got up first and shook her hand. Sandra gripped my palm carefully, though she smiled in a friendly manner.

"I look forward to hearing from you, Mrs Redlich," she said.

A moment later, we were in the common room of the office—everyone was immersed in work again.

Sandra escorted me to the front door of the office and gave me a polite smile again. I looked into her eyes, and it seemed to me that they were wet.

When I had walked out further away, the office's front door opened, and Sandra ran through it.

"Laura," she called. "I forgot to give you our business card." The woman handed me a small piece of cardboard.

I managed only to say thank you before she slammed the front door of the office.

As I drove away, I thought—a normal day, but an utterly abnormal life.

I decided to go to my parents because I hadn't visited their apartment in Riga for a long time.

I stopped the car at one of the shopping centres on the way. I sat by a window in one of the small cafes from which I could see the street. There were only a few people inside, an older man near me sipping some coffee, but he seemed immersed in reading a newspaper. He didn't even notice me. The waitress brought the menu, and I chose Caesar salad with chicken and black coffee. While waiting for food, I looked out the window and continued to think about the failed office visit. What kind of wife am I if I don't even know where my husband works?

I wanted to look at the wedding day photo again. I should show it to my parents and Paula so that they can finally tell me why they keep lying to me all the time. I had put it in the pocket of my coat that I hadn't taken off because I was tormented by cold shivers all day. Suddenly, I found that the photo was no longer in my pocket. Most likely, I forgot it in the car. But my hand touched something else—a small piece of cardboard. It was Sandra's business card.

I pulled it out and looked at it, "Sandra Lejina, VINTORS LTD, the international cargo *transportation services*." It was an ordinary business card, printed on a cheap sheet of paper. I flipped the card to see the other side.

It was handwritten. *"Laura, please don't call or come to us anymore."*

CHAPTER TWENTY-THREE

I was furious. I paid for the food I ordered and left the room, still strangling the damn business card, as if afraid that the evidence of my husband's existence might disappear as imperceptibly as my previous life.

My mother didn't answer my calls.

I had no choice but to dial Paula's number again and again, but there was no answer either. I could guess why Paula wasn't answering. My sister considered me insane and didn't want to talk to me when her influential friends and colleagues were nearby. Above all, Paula would be afraid to let them know that she has a crazy sister who has imagined a non-existent marriage.

I could no longer wait for any of them to answer my calls. I decided to go to my parents and ask—yes—this time I'll ask them to explain everything that happened.

Coming out of the shopping centre, I began walking faster. I tried to remember where I'd parked the car. When I finally found it, I sat in the car and glanced at myself in the mirror. My eyes looked sunken, my skin and hair lacked radiance. Leaning closer to the mirror, I noticed a couple of rough grey hairs. Just this morning, it seemed to me that I was looking good, despite the horrors of Agris's disappearance. Was it the stress that had suddenly made my reflection seem this awful?

My parents must know the truth. Now I had no doubt about it. However, why did they treat their own daughter so inhumanely? The issue wouldn't let me rest. I entered my parents' home address in the navigation and left the parking lot.

It was almost eight in the evening. The apartment building of the Lithuanian project in the Teika district—where my parents owned a three-room apartment—looked arrogantly at me.

I hadn't been here for ages. Since Agris and I moved to the Woodwalks, I rarely visited this place.

I had to leave my car not far from the house, right next to the gym located in a run-down, tall building. I walked up the street, crossed it and stopped at my parents' house.

I looked at the living room window. As usual, the thick curtains on the park side were open, the blue light of the TV reflected its shine on the glass. It means Dad is home and watching one of his favourite shows. I entered the staircase, climbed to the second floor, and, straightening my shoulders, rung the doorbell. The door opened quickly, and I saw a short, skinny woman staring at me in amazement. The woman had bleach blonde hair with regrown grey roots. She could have been my peer.

"Yes?" she said with no kindness in her voice, referring to me as a stranger.

"I'm sorry, I must be at the wrong door." Perplexed, I glanced at the doorplate—I wasn't at the wrong place. My parents lived here, in Apartment 16, on the second floor. "Is my father or mother home?"

"You must have confused something," she narrowed her eyes.

"No, I haven't," I replied impatiently, trying to break into the apartment. The woman stood in front of the door and called for someone. "Victor, come here! Some crazy woman is trying to break into our apartment!" the woman screamed when I pushed her and managed to enter the hallway of the apartment.

The same wallpaper, the same oak wardrobe belonged to the parents.

But where are my parents?

Around his fifties, a slightly strange guy appeared by the door with a well-visible belly and a bearded face.

"Who are you?" He referred to me, staring gloomily through his forehead.

"She broke into our apartment. I don't know her at all!" the woman shouted behind me.

"This is my parents' apartment! Where are they?" I demanded an answer as I pressed the keys on my mobile phone, hoping my parents would answer my calls and explain why these strangers were in their apartment. If my parents were here, they wouldn't miss this nonsense even if they had gone to bed early.

"Call the police," she called to the man, who was still staring at me in astonishment. "She may be a drug addict."

"You're probably saying that about yourself," I hissed back. This is my parents' apartment. I would never confuse it with any other place. I glanced at the kitchen, where my mother and I used to have dinner. The beautiful wooden table my father ordered from a famous carpenter stood in his place.

"Listen, lady. You're really confused. We have been renting this apartment for three months now, so your parents definitely don't live here. Go away before we call the cops!" the man announced in a hollow voice.

"What?" I asked in disbelief and turned to the blonde woman.

"You heard me! Walk away! We are the official tenants of this apartment!" The woman started waving a sheet of paper she had grabbed from the hallway shelf. "This is our contract! Look!"

I knew nothing about it. Strange. I tried to calm down.

"I'm sorry... I didn't know my parents rented their apartment." I apologise again, stumbling back to the front door and hold my head in shock. I was sure I'd have a migraine soon. There was a thud in my temples, almost causing me to faint, but I leaned my head against the wall.

"Oh, God, she's not well," the blonde woman ran to me and tried to keep me on my feet. "Come, sit in the kitchen. You need a glass of water." The woman suddenly changed her attitude as she seemed sorry for me.

"Maybe you'll invite her to stay with us overnight?" the man sarcastically murmured as he got angrier.

"Come with me," the woman stopped listening to the man and led me to the kitchen. "What exactly are you looking for in this apartment?"

I sat down at my father's beloved table and leaned forward, feeling like my head might soon explode. The blonde woman obviously didn't want to take responsibility if I died in the stairwell.

"This apartment…" I tried to string words. "This apartment belongs to my parents. They aren't answering my calls today, so I came to visit. I had no idea they had rented it out."

The woman frowned. She seemed to consider something.

"What are their names?"

"Walter and Mara Klavini."

"Yes, yes, that's right," she exclaimed with relief. "Then there is no misunderstanding here. I remember that the contract contained this same surname. Look at the contract," she waved it at me again. The man appeared to have accepted the presence of a stranger in their apartment and silently observed what was happening, standing by the door.

The blonde woman continued to talk about the procedures of their tenancy agreement as if something exciting had finally happened in her life.

"We found this apartment in an ad three months ago, and we signed a long-term contract. The agency took care of everything, there was no landlord on the site. But wait, the name of the apartment owner is written somewhere here. One second."

"Here it is. Klavini. The owner's name is Laura Klavina,"

the woman couldn't read any further because I tugged the contract from her hands.

"But that's my maiden name! I'm Laura Klavina," I announced, feverishly trying to read the content of the agreements, but the words blurred. The woman looked interested in what was going on and ignored the fact that I had taken her a document.

"We have the tenancy right to live here! We pay timely every month. I transfer the money to Laura Klavina, but I had no clue it's you," the man growled by my ear.

"That's impossible!"

My phone flashed again. I was hoping that my mother or father would finally call me, or at least Paula, but it was my neighbour Aya. I declined the call.

The blonde woman glanced at me curiously.

"Can you show us your passport or driver's license?" the man demanded sternly.

"I've lost my passport," I replied, and it was true. I had been desperately searching for it all over the house for several days and decided that my parents had taken it. They imagined that I am mentally ill and could lose my passport somewhere.

"I am Laura Klavina!"

"If you do not have an ID, you could be calling yourself whatever you want. I, however, see the need to call the police," the man had lost his patience.

"But if..." his wife was still trying to help.

"I told you—we must call the police!"

I got up, and the headache returned. "Please, let me use your bathroom at least. I beg you...."

Without waiting for an answer, I darted out of the kitchen, holding on to the wall. They both discussed something, but the words in my head turned into incomprehensible whispers. I turned the cold water tap and let the stream flow to my hands for a moment. I rinsed my face, and I reached for the small towel out of a habit, but instead, I grasped a wet, rough bathing sheet.

What the hell is going on here? Why don't my mother, father or Paula answer my phone calls?!

I heard the voices again, now clearly. The man had called someone.

"Yes, I told you already. She is here. She claims to be the owner of the apartment, but, in my opinion, the woman's just some local drug addict. Yes, definitely—pale, eyes red. Yes, okay."

This damn guy called the police.

For a few seconds, I stood by the mirror stiff and confused, pondering what to do. It was horrible to imagine that I would be dealing with the police again. If my father and mother find out, they will get me in the car and take me to the nearest psychiatric clinic.

The mobile phone indicated that the battery was running low. My parents had not called back, nor had Paula. Only three missed calls from Aya. What does she want from me again?

I opened the bathroom door, unable to exhale. They both stood in the kitchen and looked at me, a little scared as if I could harm them.

Without saying a word, I left the apartment and slammed the door shut with a loud noise. Perhaps they continued shouting at me from behind, but I didn't hear them anymore. I ran down the stairs, wheezing when I reached got outdoors. Tiny raindrops landed on my face, seemingly cool and gentle.

I ran around the corner without looking back and disappeared into the maze of smaller streets, trying to remember where I had left the car.

When I finally found my car and hid in its safety, I decided to look for Paula. I drove several miles—as if doing so aimlessly—but suddenly I came to my senses by Paula's house. Many new house projects hid in this green corner of the city, where apartments cost a fortune. But Paula could afford it. At the stairwell, a black cat stroked its body to my legs and disappeared. Cold chills ran down my limbs.

The man who opened the door of Paula's apartment was not particularly pleased with the unexpected guest. I didn't know him. The man was middle-aged and quite unattractive. He had worn-down jeans, a messy sweater, sports shoes dirty with white paint.

"What do you want?" he asked, standing at the door of Paula's apartment.

"I came to visit my sister. She lives here."

The man shrugged gloomily. "Unfortunately, I can't help you. I'm renovating this apartment. No one lives here yet."

"My sister lives here!" I shouted and wanted to enter the apartment, but he stood in front of the door, blocking my way.

"Girl, walk away. I have a lot of work to do. The owners are renovating this apartment, and no one has been living here for at least five weeks. I guarantee you that." And he slammed the door in front of me.

I stood in the stairwell and failed to move. The walls and ceiling seemed to fall on top of me. I couldn't believe the surprises of the last few hours, and I wanted to shout and make everything step away from me: walls, ceilings, misunderstandings, lies, threats.

Paula has moved somewhere and didn't tell me anything. My parents have rented out their apartment.

Agris is missing.

Maybe he's dead.

Despair and anger simultaneously burned a vast, hot hole in my stomach. I was afraid of my anger because I was no stranger to it. I had felt something like this once before, and it was something horrifying. I wanted to remember when and what it was, but my brain was impossible to summon.

I was able to exhale the restrained breath, which pulsated with the beats of my frightened heart. I had never felt so lonely and so sure that things would get worse in the future. There was a feeling that I would never be able to escape this nightmare, which was perhaps just a prelude, an introduction to my future life.

I rushed back home faster than sixty miles per hour. When no headlights flashed in front of me for a while, my gaze slipped to the phone. I hoped to see the missed calls from my parents. Or at least from Paula.

My body was overwhelmed by a strong sense of fear.

The driver of the van signalled loudly in the distance. My blurred gaze cleared again.

The highway. An empty, monotonous highway.

I almost missed the turn to the Woodwalks, but I was able to turn the wheel, and the car was already on the familiar road. The semi-detached houses were left behind, and I was able to notice that the lights were lit only in a few homes.

And then I saw what caused me to stop too quickly. I stopped the car and glanced at the landscape. The dark grey clouds seemed to cover the roof of the house and the ends of the trees. The lights in my house were on.

A pale yellow light moved in the hallway windows and even on the second floor. There were no parents' cars in the yard, but Paula and my parents didn't even have the house keys. Agris and I had replaced the front door. Although they were apprehensive about me and talked about the need for professional treatment, my parents respected my privacy— they wouldn't get inside on their own. Even when I was a child, my parents would never walk into my bedroom without knocking.

While I was in Riga, someone must have broken into my house. Someone crept around my home and probably collected all the valuables they could find.

Dammit, it couldn't get any worse!

I glanced at Aya's house. The windows were dark, the curtains were closed, and her car was parked in the yard. Maybe I should ask Aya for help to come with me? But I had already embarrassed myself enough, and if it turns out that I simply forgot to turn off the lights before I left, I will be the worst fool in Aya's eyes again.

Besides, I hadn't called her back, and I don't plan to do so. At least not tonight.

I started driving slowly, but I turned off the headlights to be less noticeable.

What should I do? Maybe it's better to call the police right away? What if there really is a thief in the house? Why is all this happening to me? I stopped the car at the house and watched someone show up by the windows. The light in the hallway was still on. I was hoping to see some moving body, but I didn't.

My house doesn't look tempting to thieves from the outside. The neighbour's windows were just across the road, and her car in the yard indicated that someone was living there. I almost convinced myself that I forgot to turn off the lights before leaving.

I'm probably just tired. I wiped the sweat from my face with a quivering hand. It was hot in the car. I started to feel dizzy again.

I got out and went to the house, but a bundle of keys fell out of my hands at the front door. I bent down to grasp it and heard footsteps from inside the house. Someone was walking there. More shivers run down my spine. However, I was ready to face even a criminal because I was exhausted by all this ignorance.

When I unlocked the door, I realised that it was not much warmer inside than outside. I didn't feel any wind here that would make my eyes water. I stood cautiously for a while. If there is a thief in the house, there is a possibility that he is hiding somewhere.

Carefully, I began to move forwards. Lobby, hallway, now around the corner, and I can glance into the kitchen where the light is on. Nobody's there.

Some kind of muffled noise. Steps right behind me. I'm frozen. Someone's in the house. Someone's almost standing behind me.

If I turn around quickly, will I be attacked?

A large kitchen knife came into my view. Damn, how lucky I was! Its handle shone in the sink two steps away from me. Not looking over my shoulder, I grabbed the knife, and only then I turned around, stretching the dagger right in front of me as if ready for battle.

The knife fell out of my hands as soon as I noticed him.

It just couldn't be. Am I dreaming?

"I must be looking awful," he said regretfully.

I took a few steps backwards.

Agris stood alive and well in front of me.

He spread his arms as if they were wings, and that was the only gesture my tired, hopeful heart needed to blur all the objections of my reasoning in an instant. As if sleepwalking, I slipped into Agris's embrace, pressed my face against my husband's shoulder and closed my eyes. And when his hand touched my hair, a strange, miraculous feeling took over me, as if I had just woken up. As if I had fallen asleep for a long time—not just at this point, but all the previous weeks since Agris had disappeared. But now, I had woken up and looked at my husband.

My Agris had returned home.

CHAPTER TWENTY-FOUR

The evening of the same day

The sun struggled with the fog behind the window. Henry was driving on a half-empty highway, wondering how long it would take him to find the old Woodwalks—the house which was the only indication of the woman he was looking for. Laura, the lady who has survived despite everything.

People all over Latvia talked about her tragic story not long ago. The decision was made—Henry was finally ready to meet the woman whose fate could not be indifferent to him. No prohibitions and no excuses!

Henry stopped the car at a petrol station in Pure. There was very little fuel left. If the navigation displayed it correctly, there were only a few miles left until the destination. Before getting out of the car, he wanted to look at the newspaper article again, where the information he'd found was the most accurate. The newspaper was published in May, five months ago. The pages were shabby, but the crumpled, scary photograph still wouldn't leave Henry's mind.

She lay curled on the side of the road, her head resting on the roadway like a pillow. The white bride's dress was soaked in blood. The woman's face was not visible in the photo, but Henry knew how beautiful she was.

After refilling the fuel, Henry went indoors to pay for it and buy some coffee. The salesperson reluctantly turned away from the phone screen, but she flourished with kindness, seeing the handsome man. There were no buyers in the store, and Henry took the opportunity to ask if the seller knew where the Woodwalks were located.

"You have to drive forward to the row of semi-detached houses. Then turn right, then a few miles to the place where two private houses are on both sides of the road. I don't know which one you are looking for," the seller undoubtedly flirted.

"An old, large private house, right?"

"Yes. The locals say everything is very overgrown there," the woman continued, regretfully glancing at the man who entered the store a moment after Henry.

"Thank you. I'm sure I'll find it," Henry was about to leave, but the other man stopped him.

"Are you talking about the crazy woman who lives behind the twin houses? He asked curiously. "I know her. You have to be careful."

"What are you talking about?" Henry was puzzled.

"She stole our dog. She's insane! I no longer let my wife and kids go for walks to that side! Today, she almost hit us with her car. Who even issued a driving licence to a crazy person?

Henry thanked the woman and left. It was clear that the stranger would have gladly continued to discuss Laura, but Henry was not interested in a longer conversation with him. Henry himself knew more about Laura than the stranger might think.

Six grey lone semi-detached houses indicated that the navigator wasn't lying, and there would be a turn soon. Henry drove the car in the direction of the dirt road. More than a mile of perfect dirt road. And the destination.

Henry turned off the car's loud engine and stopped a little ahead on the side of the road. He concluded that he was at the right place. Two similar private houses stood facing each other, each on its own side of the road.

A grey Passat stood by one of them. It seemed like someone could be inside that house, but a run-down wooden plate at the lonely fence post suggested that Henry should go to the opposite residence.

He pressed the doorbell at the front door at the amber brick house, and a short, old-fashioned bell rang, followed by silence.

Henry decided to look at the other side of the house, but someone addressed him from behind unexpectedly.

"What are you doing here?" The person had a calm, even velvety voice. Henry turned quickly and saw a woman in her forties eyeing him. She was wearing a business blouse and dark pants. Only her worn-down shoes indicted that this woman had not appeared from any office nearby.

"I'm looking for Laura, the owner of this house," Henry replied.

"I know you," the woman announced, blinking disdainfully. "Lauras isn't home. And you know that it's not possible to talk to her at the moment. You can use my driveway to turn your car around and leave."

Henry looked at the woman.

"And who are you, please?" he inquired calmly.

"I'm sorry?" the woman asked in surprise.

"I just wanted to know who you are and why you're making demands like a boss." Henry was unshakable.

"It's none of your business," she replied, crossing her arms.

Protection? Why? Henry smiled.

"Can we talk calmly, please?"

The woman was silent for a moment, watching Henry's face, then nodded towards her house.

"Let's go elsewhere," she called Henry, explaining, "Laura may be back soon. Come to my house, and we can have a cup of coffee, and we'll talk."

Henry nodded and followed the woman without saying a word.

"So you're her neighbour?" he clarified when they had entered the woman's house, and she pointed to a place where to put their shoes.

"Yes, you could say that," the woman replied evasively, and they went to the kitchen. She pointed at a chair and turned on the kettle, but Henry remained standing for a moment. He noticed that the kitchen space was almost empty. The glass cupboards didn't brag about stacks of plates and all those hundreds of little things that would symbolise an extended household. There were only two mugs, a coffee can and an electric kettle on the long kitchen counter. Henry wondered who this neighbour was.

"I didn't expect you to come here like this. Sorry if I sounded rude," the woman changed her tone. Her name is Aya, and she lives here alone. She's Laura's only neighbour.

Henry took a sip of Aya's coffee and waited.

"I don't want anyone to talk to her." Aya sat across from Henry and leaned her head to her right shoulder. "You know everything that happened to her? She's not really healthy. Will you take responsibility for the consequences of the questioning?"

Henry was silent for a moment.

"What do you mean by she's not really healthy?" The silence was long.

Aya smiled and took a sip. The coffee she had made was strong and with excellent taste, just like the woman who made it—too strong and elegant to live alone in such an abandoned place. Something was wrong here. Henry didn't doubt it since the moment he heard the dismissive tone of Laura's neighbour.

"What do you really want?" Aya looked straight into his eyes. The woman pursed her lips and mutely demanded an answer.

He decided to play with open cards.

"Paula... I can't forget her," Henry explained. "Time has passed, but the events don't leave my mind. I thought I should talk to Laura."

"I understand. It's like therapy, right?" Aya grinned.

"However, it is almost impossible to talk to Laura." Aya stood up and approached the window. For a moment, she looked outside as if trying to see if Laura had returned home. Disappointed, she turned to Henry but remained standing by the window. "Laura went somewhere today. It's been a long time, and she's not back yet. I'm worried. I've been calling her all day long."

"Does she live here alone now?" Henry was surprised.

"Yes," Aya replied. "But we take care of her."

"Are you her relative?"

"I'm her doctor," Aya replied calmly, looking back at the window.

There was a knock on the door, and Aya hurried to open it. Henry went after her and stayed in the lobby. He could see the other room through the open door from where he stood. There were soft cream walls, not much furniture—only a low table and a sofa that seemed like it would belong to a poor student. Everything warned that Aya probably doesn't live here permanently. The interior of the house resembled the decorations of a cinema pavilion, which can be easily installed and just as easily demolished.

Judging by the voices, a man talked to Aya in the hallway. The door opened, Aya came in with a fifty-year-old man who wore big, polished shoes.

"Are you having guests?" the man asked Aya in surprise, glancing at Henry.

"This is Henry. Paula's friend, remember?" Aya reminded him, and after a moment, the man seemed to remember something.

"Hello, Henry! I'm sorry, I didn't recognise you," he held out his big palm towards Henry. Henry was ashamed to confess, but at first, he didn't recognise the man either. It was policeman Richard Vitols—the same one who investigated the tragedy. They had met only once, the day after what happened, and it was the only conversation they ever had—short and professional. Henry didn't even remember it.

"Do you two know each other?" Henry looked at Aya in amazement.

"We could say we know each other for a long while now," Aya replied. "Richard Vitols has known Laura for years."

Henry noticed that the investigator was worried. As if knowing her were not a normal thing for him.

Richard Vitols glanced at Henry, and guessing that Henry was surprised by the presence of the investigator, he spoke, "Yes, but it really was a long time ago." After a pause, he added, "I was the one who found Laura in the woods when she was a child."

Henry widened his eyes. He remembered Paula's story of a sad event in her family when her younger sister Laura disappeared into the woods.

"It was before…"

"It was twenty-five years ago," Richard clarified. "I was in the military at the time. Still young. Laura, if I'm not mistaken, was seven years old. She was a strong girl. She survived in the woods for three days on her own. One day it was raining, the nights were cold, and it's a miracle that she didn't get pneumonia.

"Why wasn't she searched in the woods in the first place?

It's close to home," Henry asked restlessly.

"Some witness had turned the search in the wrong direction because it seemed to her that she had seen a suspicious car with a little girl standing next to it. It was later revealed that the woman had imagined everything to draw attention to herself."

"So you were the one who saved her?" Henry couldn't hide his admiration.

"Yes, it was a coincidence. A happy coincidence," Richard Vitols explained. "When I saw Laura at the police this fall, I couldn't immediately remember why she seemed familiar. When I heard her name, I realised that it was my little girl."

Henry had another question. "Did she recognise you?"

"No," Richard Vitols replied quickly. "Laura doesn't recognise me, and I don't want to evoke her childhood experiences."

Henry wanted to say something else, but Richard turned to Aya and changed the subject.

"Don't worry, Aya, this isn't the first time she's gone away on her own. In addition, she drives a car very well. Should I stay with you and wait?"

"I understand. Thank you for coming," Aya sighed with relief. "The medicine has worked, so I'm worried. We are nearing the end."

"What end?" Henry intervened, unable to hide his curiosity.

"The end is the moment when Laura will reveal the truth. It also happens in the last scenes of films, right, Henry?" Aya smiled faintly. "And the end will be emotionally difficult."

CHAPTER TWENTY-FIVE

Evening

Vigorous shivers went down the back of my spine, making me tremble. I stared at Agris blankly, watching him sit down at the table, put his hands on the white surface, and look at me as if I were the one who should give him the explanations.

"God, Agris!" I exhaled my confusion, my voice foreign. "Where have you been all this time? I almost lost my mind. You can't imagine what conspiracy theories were put into practice here. It was like a horror movie. Everyone was against me."

Agris was silent and continued to examine me. He looked the same way as he did on that damned evening when he left the house and didn't come back—the same white shirt, dark pants, sleek hair, smoothly shaved face. Agris looked as if he had come out of a fairy tale movie instead of returning home after a long disappearance.

"Where's Dodger?" I suddenly remembered about our dog. I seemed afraid to approach my husband, although I should want to kiss and caress him now. Agris didn't answer. Instead, he just smiled foolishly.

"Damn it, Agris! Talk to me!" I yelled as I couldn't stand that complacent smile. "Do you even realise what the hell I went through when you disappeared? Everyone thought I was crazy! When I tell you what the police said, you will be..."

And then he finally interrupted me.

"Laura, I've always been by your side." He looked at me with strange, dim eyes.

A bell rang at the front door.

Agris didn't move. He just kept watching me.

"Should I open the door?" The arrival of another person would only complicate everything. We should talk to each other first, but my husband pretended not to hear me as if I had to deal with everything on my own.

Someone continued buzzing the doorbell.

I stood up stiffly, slowly leaving the kitchen like I was possessed. I glanced back over my shoulder. My husband kept sitting there—for a moment, he looked like a wax figurine. I suspected that he might be ill.

The front door opened with a quiet squeak. Our neighbour Aya stood on the porch. Her gaze seemed a little worried, and at that moment, I felt the last piece of the mosaic click into place.

"Agris has returned home," I glanced at him, and she continued studying at me.

"Laura, let me come in, please," her voice sounded

reassuring, but I had to restrain myself from hitting her.

"Don't even try to talk to me right now! We will call the police immediately and get things clear. This time without your help," I shouted. "I have no idea what punishment you will be sentenced for all those lies and deceptions. But believe me, I will make sure that you are at least responsible for giving false testimony. You're working on some plan, and maybe the goal is to extort money from my husband, I…" I wanted to keep talking, but then something made me stop.

She stood still and didn't say a word. There was no shock in her expression, not even a surprise that my husband was there.

Agris was still in the kitchen, he hadn't come out to see why I was screaming. That perplexed me a bit.

"Laura, may I come in?" Aya asked as if she hadn't heard anything I said.

"It's not the right time," I said, but she shamelessly passed me by and walked into the house.

How dare she?

Aya walked into the kitchen without looking back. I had to follow her. She stood in front of Agris, who hadn't even moved.

I was overwhelmed by deep horror, not to mention the stiffening fear of what was happening. Did anything happen at all?

"Laura, she's not here," Aya walked closer and placed both hands on the back of Agris's chair. "Agris has not returned home because he has not been here for six months."

The ocean of anger returned, drowning my fear of the

supernatural things and the belief that I had entered the realm of madness.

Agris sat by the table. I only now noticed that his eyes look dead and cloudy. He just sat there, his hands weakly lowered, his head stretched forward, and then suddenly... Suddenly he was no longer there. As if I had just imagined him...

"It's gone too far," Aya said quietly. "Dear Laura... Agris is not here and has not been. He died, and your mind actually knows it. You have to accept it for your own good."

"I can't," I slowly sank into the chair. Gradually I began to grasp this—no man was sitting here a moment ago.

Or was he? What is truth, and what is a lie?

"You have to let go of what happened on the highway," Aya continued.

Finally, I took my eyes off the empty chair. I felt like a person who had regained consciousness or awakened from hypnosis.

And then I started screaming. My cries rang out and echoed brightly in the house where the dead walked. I squeezed my eyes shut with effort, veins pulsing in my temples, but I screamed and screamed. Sounds broke out of me like bells of hell and the day when my life collapsed suddenly entered the emptiness.

CHAPTER TWENTY-SIX

Aya was leaning towards me, speaking slowly and stretching the words a little. I slept in bed. For a moment, I couldn't hear her because the medicine makes me sleepy. Those were probably very powerful drugs. The effects allowed me to create a well-functioning self-defence mechanism for myself.

Aya had small shiny earrings in her ears. They caught my attention. I wanted to look at the earrings, and nothing else interested me anymore.

Aya glanced up.

"Laura? Can you hear me?"

"Agris," I said just one word that meant the whole world to me. Then I turned to the window, looked at the yard again. The magic of the shiny earrings was gone.

Aya was probably afraid that I would drown in tears as soon as I'd hear Agris being mentioned, but everything was even more complicated. I didn't understand what was happening, so I just muttered the word that expressed all my emotions lately.

"Laura, are you ready to tell me the truth?" Aya asked.

"I do not understand."

"It's time to finally stop it. You have to tell me what happened that day. Or else I will have to send you to a medical institution."

I jumped to these words. Madhouse. Psychiatric clinic for severely ill patients. I don't want to go there.

"Your consciousness has chosen to accept a different scenario."

Behind the window, heavy drops began to hit the old windowsill. The noise of heaven's tears was cleansing; it dissolved my panic—my lies soaked and melted in the rain. Aya sat down next to me and gently took my wrists.

But she didn't want to tell me the truth.

She wanted me to tell her the truth.

"It was a day you waited for many years. Wasn't it, Laura?" Aya kept holding my hands, but after a moment, she let them go and leaned back a little.

"I do not understand..."

"Your wedding day, Laura. Your and Agris's wedding day," she reminded. "Tell me what you remember from that day."

"It was a bit rainy but a happy day," I replied, and I no longer recognised my voice—it sounded so strange. "I know Agris existed."

"Agris really existed," Aya's answer followed unexpectedly and directly. Her voice sounded amazingly calm, at least I thought so.

"I already told you," I tried to object.

"However, Agris is no longer with us," Aya continued. Hesitantly, I stared at her, although I was afraid of every word that came out of her mouth.

I hate this therapy, I want it to end, although it hasn't really started yet. However, I want to understand why there are only two of my wedding day photos. Where are the rest of them? Maybe we didn't get to the registry office at all? No, that's absurd! Silly imagination.

"Your marriage was never registered," Aya continued, although I had just denied this fact in my hatred. The truth now seemed so close, the unspoken words began to tear my throat. Suddenly I could sense it—almost as if I knew what exactly Aya would tell me right away.

"Agris died on your wedding day, Laura," Aya said these words so quietly that no one else in this room could hear them. I closed my eyes, fearing what would happen next.

"Laura, you have to try to remember it. That's the only way you'll be able to accept the truth," Aya continued.

"I'm trying," I replied.

I tried. I really tried.

"It happened before the wedding ceremony," Aya continued. Her words came like a flood of poisonous wolves.

"How do you know that?" I looked her straight in the eye.

Aya got up, went to stand by the window and looked towards her house.

"We've known each other for a long time, Laura," she continued. "We met shortly after the tragedy."

Now I wanted her to shut up. The burden of memories fell

on me like the Library of Alexandria after a fire. I began to remember what had happened. Aya isn't my neighbour. I already knew her before this. She knew me.

Shut up! Do not speak! Don't say a word!

But she didn't listen to me.

"I see you're starting to remember. Good," Aya continued in a relaxed tone. "That's the purpose of the treatment. I've been increasing your dose in recent weeks, so I got worried when you drove your car. I should not have allowed that."

"I don't understand anything." Tears burst out of my eyes. Something happened to me.

Now everything seemed different.

Aya turned away from the window and looked in my direction.

"The human mind has its limits, Laura. Like our physical endurance," she continued. "You couldn't stand the pain. Your mind and consciousness refused to accept it. Such cases of schizophrenia are not uncommon. After the tragedy, you continued to live the life you wanted. But it wasn't the reality, and your consciousness refused to accept it. My job was to help you."

"What are you talking about?" I needed answers now. I had too many questions. "Who are you, Aya?"

"I'm your doctor, Laura. For almost six months," she replied calmly.

I shook my head and closed my eyes. I grabbed the pillow and pressed it to my ears.

"I don't want to remember," I shouted. The pillow muffled the sounds but not the flashes of memories.

Laughter in the yard, lots of laughter. My parents. Agris. Paula. My early childhood friend who will witness the ceremony. The driver of a beautifully decorated wedding minibus. Foggy, but I see all their faces.

"There was a tragedy that shocked the whole country," Aya continued, "and ruined your life."

I've released the pillow, and I hear exactly these Aya's words.

"No, it's a lie! Shut up, Aya!"

Shut up! Shut up! Shut up!

Aya calmly grabbed me by the shoulders and asked me to calm down.

"Laura, I'm not your enemy. I'm your friend." She looked me straight in the eye. "I'm helping you to regain your common sense and return to real life because you can't live in a nightmare. You'll perish in a fantasy world."

"My life is real!" I shouted as loudly as I could for the whole world to hear me. For Agris to hear me and return home. "Shut up!" I yelled at Aya roughly. I wanted fresh air, and it seemed like I was suffocating here. I stubbornly stood up and stared at the door.

"Laura, stop!"

Funny, but her voice didn't seem insistent at all—I could hear the notes of helplessness.

She couldn't stop me on the stairs, but downstairs I was able to look at Aya so hostilely that she even stepped back. I only had flannel pyjamas and wool socks, but I ran out in the backyard. I stopped there because I only wanted some fresh air. The gravel track was wet, so my socks got wet too. I stopped around the corner to look at the bare ash trees, the autumn brown meadows and the forest in the distance. I knelt, closed my eyes and begged my mind to return the memories.

The dirt road from the Woodwalks, the driveway on the highway, we all sit in a comfortable bus. We laugh at Dad's anecdotes, but we have to be in the registry office after half an hour. I turn my head and see a truck approaching.

A terrible thrust and one last thought—I'm probably dead.

I open my eyes and want to be alive.

Aya stands next to me and lets me lean on my knees for a while. She knows that—sooner or later—my wet feet will start to get cold, and I'll relax and get up.

"Shh", Aya exhaled, silencing my sobbing and stroking my hair. "Shh, darling. Everything is okay."

"Agris died in a car crash, but I survived." My memories have won me, and Aya holds my head in her braces.

She's silent in agreement.

Aya helps me get up, and we go home. My feet are cold, but it's tolerable—means I really feel the cold, but those trivial things are easy to save. Aya suggests making some tea. I display practicality, and I take another pair of wool socks from the chest drawers.

When Aya brought the tea, I probably appeared somewhat hopeful. She wanted to smash the last bricks in my self-defence fortress.

"The tragic car accident happened on the way to the registry office," she began. This time I listened. "The driver, your sister Paula, your parents, Agris's childhood friend and

Agris were in the wedding van. And you. Are you ready to listen further?"

"Yes," I whisper.

"The collision happened nearby. After the turn at the twin houses on the Riga-Ventspils highway. A lorry driving your way crashed into your van. Later, it turned out the driver was drunk."

I shook my head —I had to grasp what I'd just heard.

"No, don't continue," I tried to keep her from telling me the rest of it. I knew what she would say. I sensed it, but I wouldn't get over it. It would explain everything. "No, don't say it," I shouted in a full voice and reached out my hands, begging, "Please do not say they…"

"You talked to people who died, Laura," Aya continued. "Due to the psychological trauma, your mind couldn't cope with what happened. All people handle internal conversations with themselves, but everything developed into a constantly nightmarish situation for you until you completely lost control. You started to hear voices regularly. People who suffer from such conditions are convinced of their truthfulness. They see what others don't. They live with people they don't have. A person in this state is not aware that those with whom they talk don't exist. Yet they really see them. Alive and real, to whom you can ask something and get answers.

"So I'm insane."

"If someone thinks that he is more normal than the others, this fact alone causes me professional concern," Aya grinned a little. "Laura, physically, you are a strong woman. After the accident, you had a severe concussion, rupture of internal organs. For two weeks, you slept in an artificial coma, after which it gradually became clear that your mind didn't want to accept reality. I was invited to investigate your case. I consulted with other specialists, and the council decided that you should not be admitted to a psychiatric hospital. Returning home, free time, a new organism—we hoped that it would give a more favourable result. After a month and a half, you were discharged from the hospital. I had already rented a house opposite the Woodwalks, stuffed your refrigerator and kitchen shelves with food for the first time, and I even had a duplicate of your house keys. It will only be fair to let you know that my expenses and fees are paid by the father of the man who caused the tragic accident. He's not poor, so I know I'm not taking away a mouthful of bread from anyone. The drunk driver will soon be on trial. These expenses will be proof that they want to help you. The court has assessed the situation, and I've been appointed as your guardian for a while since your Aunt Astrid refused to come here from Sweden. So I'm sorry, but I had to take her place. I arranged some legal matters, rented out the apartment in your name, which your parents had left for you, and I ordered you some firewood for winter. Sometimes, when I saw you wandering further down the road, I sneaked inside your house to check if you had any food. I added the contents to your refrigerator, although I was worried it might worsen the situation.

"Did they... right away...?" I finally managed to ask because everything else Aya said was clear and understandable to me. This question arose with the greatest fear I had ever experienced, "Are my parents...?"

"Only you survived because you flew out the window after the crash. Agris's childhood friend had suffered the least, but his injuries were also incompatible with life, and he died three days later. But the rest of them... You understand what a heavy lorry is. I don't want to break your heart now by telling who died on the spot and who died on their way to the hospital, nor who passed away on the surgery table. You only managed to take pictures by the house before getting into the van to go to Tukums. Laura, they're gone, but your life goes on. They all want you to live, laugh, work, make new friends.

"They're so real, Aya." I was overwhelmed by the ocean of sadness.

I opened my sore eyes, but I couldn't turn my head. What I saw beneath me surprised me. I don't know why my beautiful wedding dress was bloody and dirty. It couldn't be fixed. Something was digging into the side of my body. I stretched my head forward and saw a piece of glass. Unbelievable that it flickered out of my right side.

It was impossible to breathe deeply because when unbearable pain would torture my stomach. My breath probably hit that piece of glass. I felt a disgusting clay taste in my mouth. I tried to pull my tongue out, but it wouldn't obey me. I was afraid to swallow sand grains. I closed my eyelids, and then peace came to me.

"Laura, they're real to you. You see them, talk to them, and they're present in your life, but it's time for you to let them go. Remember we talked about guilt? It's time to take no blame for what happened. You can only blame the person who caused the accident. Car accidents caused by drunk drivers are not a coincidence of fate. It is a murder. The culprit will be condemned."

"Why did I consider Agris missing?"

"When the medicine starts to work, one of them disappears from your mind. You no longer saw him, no longer felt him. It was easiest for you to let go of Agris, but you held on to your sister and parents in your thoughts. You continued talking to them."

"I was in Riga. Strangers live in their apartment."

"Your parents' apartment is a heritage. Tenants live there now."

"Why did the police lie to me that Agris did not exist?"

"They probably saw the personal register saying this person is dead. Everyone avoids mentally ill people— bypassing them on the roads and trying to deal with them nicely. But the inspector who spoke to you, he is my acquaintance. Mr Vitols immediately called me."

"Where are they all buried?"

"Agris and his childhood friend are buried in Gulbene, but your family is in the cemetery in Pure. You weren't at the funeral because you were in the hospital," Aya continued. "Perhaps the fact that you didn't see the funeral ceremony also contributed to the non-acceptance of reality. But after you were discharged from the hospital, taking you to the graveyard would be unwise. It would ruin your psyche even more. The funeral was a little delayed, and they were buried ten days later. I must admit there weren't many people at the funeral. Paula's boyfriend informed your parents' and Paula's friends and co-workers. Her boyfriend... Henry had to come to the wedding ceremony in Tukums, but you hadn't ever met him. After what happened, he wanted to keep in touch with you, and he even came to the hospital to visit you once, but I thought he wouldn't know how to behave in a way that wouldn't harm you, so the doctors forbade him to visit you."

"Why am I the only survivor? Why, Aya?"

Aya looked out the window and helplessly lowered her hands to the sides.

"Laura, I can only tell you about my field of knowledge. Psychiatry is a relatively new field of medicine because the human mind is harder to explore than the heart or joints. But the twists and turns of destiny seem to be unfathomable at all. All I know is that you can't blame yourself for what happened. However, while studying and treating others for many years, I have not answered why my little brother died. It is painful for people to continue living after the tragedies that divide their lives into "before and after". Everyone is trying to find the answer to the question "why". However, no one ever gets an answer.

"Why did I think I had a dog?"

"That's how you obviously saw your future with Agris. You've come up with a scenario in which, quite traditionally, the young couple gets a pet after their wedding, and then a baby appears in the family. It was your happy life that you didn't want to give up."

A happy life that we all wish to have and do not want to sacrifice.

CHAPTER TWENTY-SEVEN

"You look wonderful on your wedding day!" My mother stood in front of me and hugged me. It was a long and tight embrace—my sometimes hurried and worried mother did not hesitate to show emotions this time.

I was wearing a wedding dress with tiny beads playing in the exquisite details of the lace. When I saw the dress in a wedding fashion store, I lost my sense of time just watching it. At that time, I promised myself that I would keep the dress as proof of the happiest day of my life.

Some wedding guests paced around the backyard of our house, but the rest of them were waiting for us in Tukums. The guests were chatting with my family.

"Honey, has anything happened?" Agris stood beside me. I felt the groom's breath. He smiled. At me. At Paula. At my parents. The camera flashed, and Agris's arm was around my waist.

"Well, daughter, haven't you changed your mind?" Dad

laughed.

The words stayed with me. They were never said aloud. I couldn't admit to myself that I hadn't made the right decision. The realisation that never allowed me to rest surged forcefully.

You will never build your happiness at the expense of somebody else's disaster, my mother had told me, and I had not forgotten her words.

I knew Paula had never stopped loving Agris. I knew I had destroyed my sister's life.

"Let's go," I smiled and approached Agris. He took my hand in his palm.

"Walter and I, Paula and Maris—the maid of honour and the best man—and, of course, the bride and groom, will go to the registry office in the beautiful van," Mom informed the guests because she had carefully prepared for our wedding day. "We have to be in the registry office in twenty minutes," she added, urging us all to get in the car.

"We should've left earlier," Dad's colleague sighed, but his mistress poked her husband's soft sides.

I remember vividly what that van looked like. It was brand new, with eight passenger seats in addition to the driver's seat. Paula and Maris sat in the back, and Dad joined them. Mom sat by the window, and Agris next to her. No one was sitting next to the driver. My seat was reserved next to the groom, and I was the last one to get in.

I hesitated before boarding. Everyone noticed it. Dad joked about something to distract the guests. Agris seemed as if he hadn't noticed anything.

I got on the van.

We didn't know the driver. He was not our relative. Dad had found him while looking for a comfortable, representable vehicle in the wedding advertisements. The front of the bus was decorated with small, white roses and garlands of greenery. The driver wore a white shirt, a luxurious vest and the aroma of expensive cologne. He urged me to hurry up.

I boarded, and the driver started driving. The bus—quiet like a fish—swayed along the dirt road. Agris whispered in my ear that he was very happy, but I could only nod lightly.

I remember the sun behind the window. It was a warm spring afternoon. The rain had subsided and mercifully left us a clear sky. The sun boasted like a queen.

CHAPTER TWENTY-EIGHT

The sun was right there. Nothing had changed for the sun up there in the sky.

A moment ago, I was still sitting in the van and watching Agris, who studied the seams of his trousers. Feeling my gaze, he raised his eyes, and they suddenly widened in horror. I felt a shadow popping out in front of the road, too. The driver shrieked for some reason, and the bus turned left quickly. I also saw it with the corner of my eye—the lorry cab was dashing at us, and the giant white ghost crashed into the left side of our bus within less than a second before I slammed into the window. The last thing I felt was a forceful wave, from which the driver's body jolted towards me and strangely writhed, caught in a seat belt. Maybe it was only an illusion, but I saw Agris's frame bolting somewhere past me. His eyes stared at me as if this wasn't our wedding day but a solar eclipse.

The gravel stones on the side of the road look odd—that was my first thought when I opened my eyes. It turned out that gravel had many more colours than just dull earth tones. The wrist of my right palm was sore from the deep abrasion, and the scratches were full of tiny grains of sand. I realised I should shout, turn my head, take a breath—Goddammit—and finally understand what happened. But my breath got stuck as if it were bentgrass trying to break through a wire fence. I finally managed to move a few inches to see something more than gravel, knotweed and a ditch. A white truck was parked across the highway. The massive lorry blocked almost the whole view, but something was still visible alongside its broken cabin. I tried to pull myself closer to the edge of the asphalt, but a sharp pain struck me. I glanced down. A large glass blade glinted under my left rib. I tensed my leg muscles and tried to settle myself more comfortably—that way, I could touch the shards. I realised that it hadn't pierced too deeply— the piece wobbled. Carefully, I grabbed the chip and pulled it out, grateful it had no sharp edges. I couldn't stand any foreign object in my body. I'd never been admitted to the hospital, broken or dislocated anything—I'm a nice, good young woman who has a wedding day.

Someone was coming. I saw worn-down sports shoes, dark blue jeans; the man's pace wasn't fierce or hurried. The stranger stopped beside me. I heard some sobbing, panting, and then he fell on his knees next to me. I wanted to see the face, but I couldn't lift my head. The man lowered his hands to the ground, and I looked at his slender fingers and wondered about my ability to reason—the stranger had to be a young man because he had youthful hands with slim, trembling fingers and nails that were relatively well-groomed. A strong smell of alcohol came from the man. Suddenly I realised that this person could go back and find out what had happened.

The air brought some chatter from the surrounding people, some quick footsteps trickled nearby, screams echoed around me, but the only thing I could think of was whether my family was alive.

CHAPTER TWENTY-NINE

A week later

"Hello," Henry smiled as Laura opened the front door of her house and, looking down, seemed to be considering whether to let the stranger in. She raised her head and looked at his face. It was probably not easy for Laura to do this, but she forced herself to look around.

"I'm sorry, but I'm still doubtful if you're real," she replied, smiling weakly. "Come on in, let's have a cup of coffee in the kitchen." Henry followed Laura and took off his shoes first, then they headed for the kitchen.

"Aya said I could visit you since you're feeling better," Henry explained when Laura had offered him to have a seat. She was looking for cups and teaspoons. The movements seemed a little nervous, rather chaotic, but outwardly she seemed like a healthy woman who had finally dealt with severe emotional trauma.

"I know. Aya had already warned me that you might visit,

and I don't mind," Laura replied after a short pause. Her smile was faint, the corners of her lips slightly trembling—still better than nothing.

"How are you?" Henry asked when Laura sat down at the table, and they both sipped some coffee.

Laura raised her head. Henry saw that something had changed in her face, but it was several moments before he noticed that wrinkles of pain had appeared on both sides of Laura's nostrils.

"It's getting better. I don't see them anymore. I haven't spoken to them," Laura replied. "Looks like I'm not going to the madhouse, after all.

"Laura, you have no reason to feel uncomfortable in front of me," Henry added sensitively. "You went through a huge tragedy."

"You lost a person close to you, too," Laura added. "However, you don't have seizures and schizophrenia. The whole Pure thinks I'm crazy. And I thought the world around me was in turmoil…"

"I loved your sister, Laura," Henry admitted. "We were together for a short time, only a few months, but she was a woman I would like to marry."

He didn't lie. Sooner or later, he would have married Laura's sister, and they would have children.

He learned about the tragedy from the newspapers.

A horrific car accident took place on Ventspils-Pure highway. Members of the same family died in a car accident caused by a drunk driver.

Paula had invited Henry to her sister's wedding, but two

days before the planned event, the company's management sent Henry on a business trip abroad. In Hamburg, the pace of his work was busy, but every night he tried to call Paul with no success. She couldn't be reached. In the evening, when Herny arrived in Riga, the news about Paula and her family's fate shattered his heart and mind.

"Do you remember the funeral, Henry?" Laura interrupted Henry's memories.

A terrible scene suddenly appeared before Henry's eyes as three coffins were laid in one family's cemetery.

"Let's not talk about it. But half a year has passed. We can go to the cemetery together if you want. I've been there several times since what happened."

She nodded lightly.

Henry put his palm on her hand and pressed it lightly. The touch was short, yet long enough for his nerves to tense like under an electric shock, and for a moment, Laura was the only thing he could see—her hair, her mouth, and her eyes. Damn, she reminded him of Paula so much. He had promised himself for months that he would come to visit Laura. But the realisation that he would talk to Paula's sister tormented him. Henry knew that Laura no longer had anyone. She had lost her entire family, and the only person who was really worried about Laura's health was her doctor, Aya, and that old investigator. Henry should've had arrived earlier, but he hadn't.

"I'm going to sell the house and move to my parent's apartment in Riga. I've already informed the tenants," Laura shook her hand and changed the subject of the conversation.

"That is great. Are you planning to return to work?" Henry was really interested.

"Yes, I think so," Laura replied. "Aya won't live here anymore. It turns out that she rented the house just to take care of me. The family whose drunk son caused the accident paid Aya for my treatment.

"Yes, I heard that man's father was wealthy," Henry added. "However, it didn't help in court. The guy got fifteen years in prison."

"He not only ruined his life but also wiped out several lives," Laura added.

There was silence again. This time it was dead quiet. They both seemed reluctant to speak.

"Okay, Laura, I have time to return to Riga," Henry thanked her for the coffee and got up. "But I'm happy I met you."

Laura smiled at him and escorted him to the front door.

"Henry, I really enjoyed talking to you. If you have time, come visit me again."

"Of course," Henry turned to leave but stopped at the door. "Listen, Laura, why don't we go somewhere together?"

Laura felt stunned for a moment.

"Why?" she asked in amazement.

"You'd benefit from a rest, sitting by a pond in a cafe. And you would benefit from a good company. What do you think?" Henry offered again.

Laura considered for a moment. Then she pursed her lips with a smile and nodded in agreement.

"I could really do with a good company. Unless you are

ashamed to go to the city with a woman whom the locals consider crazy," Laura added.

Henry shook his head and laughed. "You can't even imagine how little I care of what others think of us."

As they got into Henry's car and drove off the highway, Henry noticed Laura tightening her seat belt. They hardly talked while driving. In the centre of Tukums, Henry lazily drove through a couple of streets until he found a cafe. He parked the car and looked at Laura questioningly, and Laura nodded in approval.

People hurried past them. The sky was grey, but Henry was in a good mood and hoped that Laura's spirit would improve, too.

Unbelievable, but she is healed, and her life is back to normal. The pain of what happened will definitely hurt for the rest of her life, but it will be better than hallucinations and nightmares. Time will heal her. Now a beautiful woman is walking next to Henry, and there is no evidence of the horrible tragedy of her life.

The cafe was full, and loud flocks of young people were sitting at the tables. Henry found the only free table in the far corner of the cafe and noticed that Laura was worried, entering the crowd. She avoided looking around.

"Don't think about what others will think," Henry whispered, carefully placing his hand on Laura's back and directing her toward the free table.

When they had taken off their coats and sat down, a waitress came to them. Laura asked for Caesar's salad and fruit tea. Henry ordered black coffee and English breakfast, even though it was noon. It was his favourite dish.

"I'm sorry," Laura muttered to break the moment of silence between the two of them. "They probably don't know me. But knowing that everyone in small towns knows about each other, I have this feeling like they're pointing the finger at me every time I turn my back."

"Speaking of strangers," Henry leaned forward, crossing the fingers of both hands, and Laura noticed that his eyes were shimmering. "Studies show that people think about life events of strangers for a very short time. Eighty per cent of the time, a person focuses only on what is going on in their own life, so you have no reason to worry."

"Thank you for inviting me to recollect my thoughts," Laura smiled and looked at Henry." It is a pleasure to be with someone who knew my sister."

The waitress brought the drinks, and Laura added sugar to her tea. Henry examined her without looking away.

"Listen, Laura, I don't know if you want to talk about it, but maybe I should tell you something," Henry said.

"What?" Laura looked up anxiously, and their gazes met again. Laura pursed her lips.

"Your sister loved you very much." Henry started. "When we started dating, everything quickly became very serious, although at first, Paula was evasive. Later, she admitted that you had seduced her ex-boyfriend," Henry thought it was foolish to talk about it, but intuition said in advance that it was important for Laura to hear it.

"Please go on," Laura added quickly, confirming Henry's suspicions.

"There is not much to say. At first, Paula thought she would never talk to you again, but then she realised that it was the best thing that had happened, because that's how she met me. Paula often said that despite everything, she loved her sister. I thought it would be important for you to hear it."

Laura was silent for a moment. She blinked, looked at the bar, and her gaze returned to Henry.

"Thank you, Henry," she said. "It was incredibly important for me to hear that. And it is painful for me that your future with her got also destroyed.

"Me too, Laura," Henry smiled sorrowfully. "But we both need to move on."

An unsettling expression appeared on Laura's face. It seemed to Henry that she was thinking about her deceased family again. Maybe she's just wearing a comfortable face mask and doesn't stop thinking about them at all.

"Paula wasn't the first important person in my life I lost," Henry suddenly admitted.

Laura looked at Henry.

"My brother died when he was only twenty," Henry admitted. "It ruined our family. My father and mother are still together, but some things can no longer be fixed. Laura, when you say people are pointing the finger at you and you're worried that someone may consider you crazy, you're wrong. Millions of people have experienced similar sorrows and could relate.

"I'm so sorry you had to lose your brother," Laura added sympathetically, and Henry noticed that she had barely touched the salad she had ordered.

- It's okay. Many years have passed now," Henry added and changed the subject swiftly. He didn't want to go back to his memories. "Look, it says here that there will be a musical performance here tonight." Henry pointed at the advertisement leaflet by the salt jar. "Shall we stay?"

"I don't know, Henry," Laura said doubtfully. "I haven't danced..."

"You don't have to dance. We could simply sit and enjoy the performance," Henry suggested. "And then I'll take you home afterwards."

Laura glanced at her watch and reluctantly turned her head.

"I don't think it's a good idea, Henry," she continued, but Henry stretched his hand lightly and put it on hers.

"Just a few hours. Music has never hurt anyone."

"Okay," Laura's smile finally appeared, and she nodded lightly. "But not for too long."

Later, they ate pizza and drank a bottle of wine. Laura only sipped it, so Henry drank most of the wine and promised to take Laura home by taxi. The icy coldness from Laura gradually began to fade. They walked out of the cafe, and Henry smoked a cigarette. The lights above Tukums flickered like it was a summer night, music kept roaring indoors, and a loud murmur could be heard from inside. Henry smoked and studied Laura. She wasn't even intoxicated, but she seemed to enjoy herself. The smiling people she was trying to avoid a few hours ago were close to her now, passing by and behaving loudly. And at least it didn't bother Laura tonight.

In the taxi on the way back to Pure, they were silent again. The passionate conversations between the two had subsided. Each of them was now sitting on their side in the back seat.

CHAPTER THIRTY

A month later

Henry stopped by Laura's house. He got out slowly. A strong, warm spring wind hit him in the face. For a moment, he stood and viewed the place where he had met Laura a month ago. At that time, they had spent a great evening in Tukums. Henry hadn't felt so free and relaxed for a long time talking to a woman.

They had called each other almost every day for the past three weeks. The conversations sometimes lasted for several hours. Maybe they only used the bond that could never be broken as an excuse—the connection to Paula. Now Henry was finally ready to end the protracted situation. They were no longer children or teenagers but two lonely people in their thirties who kept an imaginary distance solely for the sake of Paula's memory.

Henry realised that Laura's situation was even worse. It was she who once took Agris away from her sister, and for many people, Henry and Laura's closeness after Paula's death would seem absurd and unacceptable. How could she deprive her sister of a man even after her sister's death?

Henry had thought about it for hours until he finally realised that he had trained Laura to ignore what others thought.

Hell, they both had to live on.

Laura didn't answer the phone for three days and didn't use social media anymore, so Henry decided to visit her and ensure she was fine.

Henry rung the doorbell. He kept standing there for a while because no one came to the door, although there were footsteps inside the house.

Wasn't she home? Henry glanced at the yard and made sure he wasn't hallucinating—Laura's car was really by the house. Maybe she's in the shower or cooking and not hearing Henry's knocks? Maybe the doorbell doesn't work? He knocked again.

He had already decided to step through the window to make sure that Laura was okay, but she finally showed up by the hallway window next to the front door. Laura opened the curtains and studied the guest.

"Laura, it's me, Henry. Please open the door." Henry walked over to her and smiled, but he didn't like the look on Laura's face. She seemed like she hadn't closed her eyes the entire night. Laura muttered something, then disappeared from view, and Henry heard the footsteps inside the house again. However, after a moment, the key clicked, and finally, she opened the door.

Henry stood outside, staring at Laura's surprised expression. Now he was confident that something had happened. His attention was drawn to Laura's eyes—reddened eyelids and dark circles under her eyes.

An uncertain smile slowly appeared on her face, and the young woman said, "Good afternoon! How can I help you?"

She was wearing a simple red shirt, jeans and slippers, and her hair was carelessly put in a high ponytail.

"Laura... It's me!" Henry squinted in surprise. Why did she behave this way?

"I'm sorry, but I don't know you. Has anything happened?" Laura looked at Henry with puzzled eyes. She didn't even open the door wide enough, seemingly threatened by Henry like he was a stranger she saw for the first time. Henry wasn't sure what to reply—it was clear that Laura wasn't joking. She didn't know Henry. And then it hit Henry like a dull, heavy object. Once again, she was...

"I'm looking for Agris," Henry suddenly announced, waiting for Laura's reaction. "I'm his acquaintance."

"Oh!" Laura laughed carelessly. "Why didn't you say so right away? Unfortunately, Agris isn't home at the moment. He's gone to work. Has anything happened?"

"No, no, it's all right. I just passed by and thought he would be home. I'll call him later, thank you." Henry retreated quickly, still stunned by what had happened.

"Do you have his phone number?" Laura took a step forward, continuing to study the stranger. "Maybe I'll call him and tell him that a guest is waiting for him?"

"No, no, that won't be necessary," Henry replied,

glancing at the neighbouring house, where he saw Aya standing in the yard. She stood there with her arms crossed, staring at Henry.

"Why don't you come in for a cup of coffee and wait for Agris to return?" Laura offered again.

"No, really, thank you," Henry turned quickly and went to the car. Aya waved at him, inviting him over.

"What's your name?" Laura's question came from behind.

Henry stopped and turned to Laura.

"Henry. My name is Henry," he replied.

"Nice to meet you, Henry! Visit us!" Laura turned around, and her dark hair fluttered in the air, but the light from her house flickered. The key made a locking sound twice, and Laura was gone.

Henry reclined both hands on the side of his car and stayed there for a moment, unable to figure out what to do.

Aya. She was still standing by the house. Henry got into his car and drove to Aya's yard. He got out of the car, looked back at Laura's house to see if she was near the windows. Henry opened his mouth, not knowing what words would flow from it, but before he could speak, Aya's hand grabbed him by the shoulder.

"Henry, I warned you," Aya whispered calmly. "I warned you that Laura's ill."

"Why didn't she recognise me? I thought she was better for the past few weeks," Henry shouted in irritation. "Just three days ago, we talked for hours every night. She planned to return to work, preparing to sell her house. I helped her find a good agent."

"No, Henry. Come in before she notices us," Aya invited, and Henry followed her. He stopped in the hallway when Aya had closed the front door and immediately asked for an explanation.

"Damn, she doesn't know who I am, and she's talking about her husband again," both resentment and pain echoed in Henry's voice.

Aya agreed and nodded.

"Did you really think it was that simple? Feed a person with strong drugs and cure them in a few weeks?" Aya blinked and looked intently at Henry. She sat down in a chair in the hallway and crossed her arms again. "Henry, I should've told you right away."

"What are you talking about?" Henry eyed her, feeling more and more nervous.

Aya forced a faint smile and continued, "Laura will be looking for her missing husband for the third time this year."

Henry didn't know how to react.

"Henry, did you really think this is the first time something like this has happened? Every time the treatment takes effect, one of her family members begins to fade from her mind. They disappear because they haven't been there for a long time. Her family is dead, but the medicine stops her hallucinations. She can't deal with it, she can't explain it to herself, so her mind assumes that her loved ones go missing. She feels as if her mind has flown away somewhere. It is schizophrenia with nightmare ideas if you want an accurate diagnosis. Henry, this is a struggle that I must go through over and over again. Every time it seems that it may be the last time, it turns out that this story is no fairy tale. In real life, schizophrenia is a mental illness that's difficult to treat.

Henry shrank a little, and suddenly he wanted to smash his left fist into the grey walls of Aya's house.

"What's going on with her now?" He asked in a recollected voice. "She is such a young woman."

Aya shook her head doubtfully.

"Laura believes that her husband has gone to work and she is waiting for him at home. Maybe she's calling her parents or sister again and talking on the phone for hours with audible beeps on the other end of the call. Agris will probably disappear soon, and she will look for him again. In any case, my time here is over. I have to return to Riga."

"Are you kidding me?" Henry frowned in confusion. "She's not healthy. Who will take care of her?"

"The municipality is informed about everything, as well as the medical council. Laura has a sick leave. She will not be left alone, Henry. I can't dedicate several years to one patient. I have other patients in Riga."

Henry revisited the memories of the recent weeks, playing them out like a movie in his head.

"It can't continue like this, Aya. She was a completely normal and logical woman until today. It must be stopped immediately. I will take her to her husband's and family's grave..."

"Henry, I understand that it may seem like you're smarter than doctors, but if things were so simple and we could deal with such illnesses quickly, psychiatric hospitals would have been closed a long time ago. Let us doctors do our job, and I will only be grateful if you continue to support Laura and take an interest in her health."

"I'll pay as much as it's needed," Henry offered. "Please stay here and continue to treat her."

Aya smiled as if she had just met a good friend.

"It's not necessary, Henry." Aya stood up. "The family of the guilty driver who caused the tragic car accident would gladly continue to pay me in the future, but, as I said, I have to return to Riga, where I have scientific work and other patients waiting for me. Laura has become very close to me; maybe I even broke the distance between the patient and the doctor and grew to love her as a child I've never had. Her tragedy also reminded me of my own childhood trauma, and I sincerely wanted to help her, but I can't keep doing it for the rest of my life."

"I understand," Henry slumped on the other chair in the hallway. "What would you suggest I do? I want to help her."

"Then wait. Just wait, Henry," Aya's answer didn't sound hopeful. "Only time can heal all wounds. I have used many different medications to treat Laura. Now it's time to wait."

"Honestly—how long do you think this will last?"

"I don't know, Henry. I can't answer that question. Maybe the day will come when she lets them go. Then it will get better."

Henry avoided looking at the window that had a view of Laura's house. Turning away helped him to overcome the desire to return to Laura and tell her the whole truth. Aya's right. How will she perceive it? Laura believes Agris has gone to work and her parents are alive and well.

When Henry turned towards the window again, he saw Laura standing in the kitchen. She looked directly at him.

Aya came closer and noticed the same thing.

"She's watching me," she explained. "To dispel loneliness, she's been watching my every step for months. Every week she bakes a pie or a cake and comes to see me," Aya continued. "It makes my work a little easier and helps me give her medicine, but it only works temporarily. And during that time, she can't figure out what's going on with her. Someone in her family disappears. Literally disappears. And she feels like they're all plotting against her. Two local families have already left their homes in recent months because they cannot live with Laura. In the fall, she stole a neighbour's dog, claiming it belonged to her and her husband."

Cold shivers ran down Henry's back.

The wind danced outdoors, but the world turned to eternal greyness again. White? Black? Where was it? Was it Laura's in mind?

*"We can only be said
to be truly alive in
those moments when
our hearts are
conscious of our
treasures."*
— Thornton Wilder

CHAPTER THIRTY-ONE

Two years later

At night, I experienced the worst nightmare I had ever seen. I woke up on my birthday after midnight and concluded that there was a deep night outside the window, and only the dim moonlight helps me see my body. What I saw in my nightmares seemed genuine and frightening. It was as if my mind had flown somewhere and left my body like an empty shell. In the nightmares, I saw my husband and the rest of my family dead. There was a tragic car accident on the morning of our wedding day. A stranger's lorry on the highway crashed into our van with my family and me inside. It seems like I survived only because I woke up from the dream. But it felt like they died.

I turned on the dim night lamp. I stayed awake, trying to get rid of my thoughts.

The nightmares seemed so real. As if it had actually happened.

Because it did happen.

Because I remembered it. My family died. I survived.

I heard footsteps on the first floor of my house. They came from the kitchen. Anxious, I got out of bed and slid my feet into the soft slippers. The moon still ruled the purple sky behind the window.

I went down to the first floor in quiet, slow steps and stopped by the kitchen door.

My family had gathered in there in the middle of the night as unexpected guests.

Mom vigorously kneaded the dough for the cake on the stove, Dad sat at the kitchen table and read a newspaper. Agris was seated at the table, viewing me with a puzzled gaze, but Paula was sitting next to him on the stool. Her eyes rose towards me when she noticed me entering the kitchen.

Paula smiled. Moonlight covered her skin like gilded silver.

"Laura, will you join us for dinner?" Dad removed his glasses and put the newspaper on the table. "Your mother has made a roast, and there will be a delicious cake for dessert."

"Same as on your wedding, darling," Mom exclaimed happily, continuing to knead the dough.

"Laura, is everything okay?" Agris got up and slowly approached me.

"I have no appetite," I replied.

I wanted to continue to be with them even when the whole world thought I was insane. It has never been more challenging to make a decision.

I turned on the light. There was no one in the kitchen.

They're gone. I'm here. And one day we will meet again. But not now.

Perhaps each of our birthdays is an invitation from God to live on.

The end

Dear readers,

While writing this book and researching the subject, I learned that the statistics of drunk drivers on the roads are harsh in many countries.

The most dramatic statistics refer to those drivers caught under the influence of more than 1.5 per mile, hence heavily intoxicated.

For the accident prototype in which the whole family lost their lives, I used a real event from a tragic car accident in Estonia in 2020, when a 34-year-old driver caused a car crash under the influence of almost 3.7 per mile. People in the same family lost their lives: the driver was a 27-year-old woman, her 58-year-old mother and the driver's daughter was only an 8-months-old. The only one who survived the accident was a 37-year-old woman—the driver's sister. She lost her entire family.

Accidents caused by drunk drivers are not destiny or tragic accidents. Drunk drivers are potential murderers. I call for condemning driving under the influence of alcohol. I am convinced that we, as a society, can actually influence more than we think.

With love,
Lelde Kovalova

Thanks for reading. If you enjoyed this book, please consider leaving an honest review on your favorite store.
The author will be very grateful.

Sending you sunshine to brighten your day.

Made in the USA
Monee, IL
15 December 2021

85412413R00115